Henry Augustin Beers

A Suburban Pastoral

And Other Tales

Henry Augustin Beers

A Suburban Pastoral
And Other Tales

ISBN/EAN: 9783337072568

Printed in Europe, USA, Canada, Australia, Japan

Cover: Foto ©Andreas Hilbeck / pixelio.de

More available books at **www.hansebooks.com**

"About cock-crow they passed through a little town." —Page 51

UBURBAN
PASTORAL

And Other Tales

BY

HENRY A. BEERS

NEW YORK

HENRY HOLT AND COMPANY

1894

CONTENTS.

		PAGE
I.	A SUBURBAN **PASTORAL**, . . .	1
II.	A MIDWINTER NIGHT'S DREAM, .	33
III.	A COMEDY OF ERRORS, . . .	65
IV.	DECLARATION OF INDEPENDENCE, .	119
V.	**SPLIT** ZEPHYR, ...	149
VI.	A GRAVEYARD IDYL, . . .	205
VII.	**EDRIC** THE WILD **AND** THE WITCH WIFE, ...	247
VIII.	**THE** WINE-FLOWER, . . ⟩	257

I.

A SUBURBAN PASTORAL.

A SUBURBAN PASTORAL.

N their walks about Southwick it was often agreed between Sproat and Clitheroe that the one or the other of them ought to have an uncle living somewhere in the environs. But each insisted that the duty of providing him lay with the other : Clitheroe on the ground that he had come to town several months the later and was therefore a comparative stranger ; Sproat because, as he maintained, Clitheroe carried about him nepotic suggestions.

"You look like a man with lots of uncles," said Sproat, "and I don't."

It must be acknowledged that the credit of inventing this avuncular fable belonged to Sproat. It happened of a windy March twilight, when Clitheroe looked at his watch and said :

"Quarter of six. Come, we must be getting back to the boarding house."

"Now," answered Sproat, who was balancing dreamily on the top rail of a fence, "if you only had an uncle somewhere out this way, with a well-stocked sideboard and a lot of pretty daughters ! Then we could fetch up at his house and take dinner, and spend the evening around the fire. And about —— G. M., when

we were good and sleepy, the **old** gentleman would have the hired man hitch up and drive us in. Wouldn't that be better than tramping back **to** Mrs. Barker's cold meat and stewed prunes **?** Why don't **you** have an **uncle,** Clitheroe ? "

The pleasing **fiction** thus propounded soon took on the proportions of a full-grown myth. Fancy added detail to the picture of this imaginary uncle, until the idea of his life did sweetly creep into their study of imagination ; and his household, his generous mahogany, his stables, hothouses, and wide verandas acquired a certain definiteness. At times they would pause before the gate **of** some uncommonly inviting villa, and exclaim: "What **a** place for an uncle ! "

In the absence **of** the real article they went as far as to discuss the feasibility of creating an artificial one. Adopting a hint from the catalogue of the Neophogen University, they wondered whether it might not be possible to hire some " learned man who had failed in business," rent a convenient country house, and set him up as an uncle. His sole duty would be to dispense an open hospitality to his nephews, from resources secretly provided by themselves. But this scheme was too expensive to be seriously thought of. It remained a beautiful dream.

The two friends had few acquaintances in Southwick. They had come to the little city not long before—Sproat to take the position of

chemist in the dye works, Clitheroe as designer
of patterns to a carpet-weaving establishment.
Accident had brought them to the same boarding house, and intimacy resulted from their
common fondness for walking—an old-fashioned
exercise which they preferred to swinging clubs
and putting up dumb-bells in the Y. M. C. A.
gymnasium, or even to knocking a ball over a
net in the tennis court which Mrs. Barker's
boarders had laid out in the back yard. Except
on Sundays, however, business kept them too
close to permit of their straying very far afield.
Having only an hour or two free at the end of
the afternoon, they had to content themselves
usually with exploring the streets and outskirts
of the city.

There is one glory of the country and another
glory of the town, but there is a limbo or ragged
edge between which is without glory of any
kind. It is not yet town—it is no longer country. Hither are banished slaughter pens,
chemical and oil works, glue factories, soap
boilers, and other malodorous nuisances. Here
are railroad shops and roundhouses, sand lots,
German beer gardens, and tenement blocks.
Land, which was lately sold by the acre, is now
offered by the foot front; and no piece of real
estate is quite sure whether it is still part of an
old field or has become a building lot. Rural
lanes and turnpikes have undergone metamor-
phosis into "boulevards," where regulation
curbstones prophesy future sidewalks, and
thinly scattered lamp-posts foretell a coming

population. Far out on sandy plains the ear
is startled by the tinkle of horse-car bells;
and the eye descries this moving outpost of
civilization making **its** way along a track bordered with ragweed and daisies, conveying a
dejected driver and a solitary fare to some
remote destination a mile or two beyond city
limits. Here is **a** smart new corner grocery in
red brick, center of a growing trade, and deriv-
ing its patronage from rows of little new wooden
houses, to whose front yards and turf borders
the lawn mower and the rubber hose have already
given a municipal smugness. The frequent
baby carriage and the swarms of children hanging upon the music of that suburban minstrel,
the organ grinder, justify the enterprise of the
grocer and the faith of the real estate specu-
lator. On the opposite corner is a decayed
farmhouse, with its cow sheds and outbuild-
ings. Perhaps a pile of milk cans decorates the
farmyard, and a half dozen cows still graze the
neighboring pasture. But more likely the cows
have disappeared, and pasture and orchard—
where a few surviving apple trees stretch their
naked arms to heaven—have passed into un-
fenced lots intersected by diagonal paths, short
cuts of tin-pailed mechanics; bediamonded in
the center by local ball nines, who play the
national game there on Saturdays (and eke, it is
to be feared, on Sundays); and browsed by the
goat—cow of the suburb.

As they grew familiar with this outcast region,
our peripatetic philosophers found a picturesque-

ness in its peculiar scenery. At least Clitheroe did, and secretly perhaps so did Sproat, although he professed insensibility and flouted the rhapsodies of his companion, whom he accused of *Schwärmerei* and of getting points of view from Mr. Howells' " Suburban Sketches."

" Come, now, Clitheroe," he would say, " there's an old hen-house with the sunset shining through the laths ; and there's an abandoned omnibus, and two or three red cedars, and some ducks in a puddle in the foreground, and two niggers with a scoop-net going across the middle distance. Can't you get up some fluff about that ? *Effet de soleil* or something ? Come, give us a frenzy !"

Clitheroe said that he liked the new corner grocery and the rows of fresh-painted Queen Anne cottages, and even the wandering horse car and empty boulevards. They were raw, but they were signs of growth—emblems of the young, hopeful, expansive American spirit. At the same time he enjoyed the pathos which attended the retreat of rural aristocracy before the advance of urban democracy. There were, in the circuit of their rambles, two or three mansions of ancient gentility stranded high and dry among squalid surroundings. One in particular, which had once been a gentleman's country seat and was now a tenement house occupied by several Irish families, stood on a hill which the new boulevard had cut through, leaving a bank of red clay. Twenty feet overhead the gravel walk ended in air, with its

flanking box borders, whose bitter aroma recalled the past. The turf had slipped away
from the terraces; the horse-chestnuts and
weeping willows were dead or dying; the snowberry and althæa shrubs lived **a** scraggly life;
and behind the big wooden columns of the
portico, many-colored garments fluttered on **a**
clothes line. Yet with something **of** the air of
a Greek temple on its acropolis, or of a feudal
castle from its steep, the old house looked down
upon the intruding squalor: upon the line of
dump carts tilted up against the bank, where
Italian laborers were at work upon the new
reservoir; upon the cinder heaps and rank
Jamestown-weeds and tomato-cans of the
neighboring lots; upon the gang of hoodlums
lazily working the growler on the doorstep of a
contiguous shanty.

All these appreciations Sproat greeted with
scorn. Yet twice **or** thrice a week, between
four and five in the afternoon, he would present
himself at the door of his friend's room, walk-
ing-stick in hand, and challenge him to a consti-
tutional.

"Don't you want to *rôder autour* the pur-
lieus a bit? There's that obsolete toll-gate on
the Wellsville road **we** were going to visit
again—the one you romanced about the other
day—where we got the home-made root beer.
Or the blacksmith's shop, where you thought
you saw Vulcan kindling up the Cyclopean
forges. Cut work for an hour or so; you'll do
it all the better this evening."

And Clitheroe would look up from his drawings and laugh, and presently reach for his hat and stick, and the two would set off in search of fresh discoveries.

Quite as often as not it happened that Clitheroe, on his way home after business hours, called for Sproat at the laboratory.

"Come," he would say, "you old dyer's hand. Your nature is subdued to what it works in. Come out into the light of things."

On one such occasion, when the April day was declining toward a pale sunset, and the incessant ring of the hylas from ponds and wet meadows brought that touch of melancholy which sounds a minor note in the promise of our belated springs, as they turned into the street from the gate of the Excelsior Dye Works, Sproat said:

"Are you particular about getting back at six? I feel like covering a little more ground to-night. Suppose we cut the boardin'-'us and get supper somewhere about eight o'clock."

"All right," responded Clitheroe. "I'm with you. Which way is it?"

"How's the Wellsville pike?"

"A chestnut. You haven't the least originality."

"No, but I have a thirst on me that I wouldn't take five dollars for, and nothing but Hiram's sassafras vintage can quench it."

"Very well; the Wellsville pike be it, then. I'm weak to-night. I've got the spring languor and can't wrangle with a disputatious cuss."

Half an hour later they were at the little way-side house by the extinct toll gate: a spot which always appealed to Sproat by its beer and seed cakes, and to Clitheroe by its quaintness. The frame of the gate still bestrode the highway, a relic and survival which Clitheroe compared with Temple Bar. Even the idle gate had not been taken down, but was swung open and lashed to the roadside post, reminding the traveler of an old hulk tied up to rot by Lethe's wharf. A board with faded letters still proclaimed the **tariff** for single and double teams and parties on horseback.

"What a bully old anachronism it is!" was Clitheroe's comment. "I don't know why a toll gate always makes me think of an elopement."

"No more do I," answered Sproat, "nor why anything makes you think of anything. Your law of association of ideas is morbidly eccentric."

The cake and beer were administered unto them by a lank but genial Yankee, with high cheek bones and a goaty wisp of beard under his chin, who was known to our perambulators as Gosh-Darn-It, but whose baptismal name and orphaned state were blazoned on a sign-board over the door:

Hiram, the widow's son, I hope,
Can furnish customers with soap
Such as can make a washing day
Pass off as pleasant e'en as May.

Leaving the toll-gate, they passed a **region** of brick-kilns, and then **a pond** with a row **of** ice-houses, whose **high-pitched** roofs Clitheroe noted as an instance **of early** Gothic ; and **whose** various tints of wood-color, grading from a weather-beaten gray **to** a fresh pine yellow, Sproat remarked as resembling the annual rings **in the** trunk of a tree, and furnishing **a** gratifying evidence of the yearly growth **of** the ice trade. Beyond the ice-houses they crossed **a** railroad cut, which **had** hitherto formed the limit of their walks in this direction, and struck into an unfamiliar country.

It was growing dusk when they stopped in front of what seemed an old-fashioned country residence, somewhat run down at **the** heels. The house had **a** Southern look; **at** least so thought Clitheroe, who had never been farther south than Philadelphia. At any rate it was low and rambling, only a story and a half high, **with** many dormer windows, and a veranda **around** three sides. Clitheroe also said that it recalled to him—he did not quite know why— some **vague** old lines which he went on to recite :

> "I walked upon the winding shore,
>   I gazed upon the ocean's foam,
> I listened to the wild wind's roar,
>   And then—oh, then !—I thought of home."

"Vague old lines!" snorted Sproat. "You made them **up** yourself, you **dog,** and now you are getting them off on me without the shadow of an excuse. You haven't even led the conversation up **to** them. What has this house got to do with ocean foam ?"

"The gateposts," pursued Clitheroe, "are a trifle too pretentious, but I observe with approbation **the** circumstance that one of the stone urns is ruinous."

A light **or two began to** glimmer in the windows.

"**How** would **that do for** an uncle ?" asked **Sproat.**

"Pretty well," answered Clitheroe doubtfully, "**It** isn't quite my ideal. I had thought of the uncle's establishment as having a rather more modern and prosperous air—rather more upper works, for one thing—cool, airy chambers for the casual nephew. This, now, is 'picturesquee'—as the Vulgarian Atrocity at Mrs, Barker's would say—but is it practical ?"

"But a quiet, inexpensive uncle——" suggested Sproat.

"A little uncle for a cent—" agreed Clitheroe.

"Or haply an aunt——"

"The very place for an aunt !"

"Come on," exclaimed Sproat, seizing the other by the arm and starting toward the house ; "something tells me that there is an uncle of some kind in there, and I am going to see."

"I'm in it," responded his friend, and arm in arm they entered the gateway and advanced up the weedy gravel walk. But presently it became evident to Clitheroe that Sproat was going through with the adventure in earnest. He marched grimly **and** silently to the **door** without relaxing **his** hold upon his companion, **who** began to have misgivings. For a moment **the** thought even occurred **to him** that Sproat might have put into practice their Utopian project of hiring an uncle, thus preparing for Clitheroe a pleasant little surprise. **But** this notion he rejected as **wild.** Meanwhile Sproat, who had been fumbling for the bell, had found it **and** given it a pull, and **a** startling tintinnabulation rang through the hall.

" What the devil ! "—Clitheroe at last broke silence, struggling to pull away his arm.

" Keep shady—keep shady ! " remonstrated Sproat, holding on firmly ; and suddenly **the** door was thrown open, **a** flood of light streamed out, and Sproat **was** saying to the housemaid :

" **Are** Mrs. **Venable and the** young ladies in ? "

" Oh, my prophetic soul ! Your uncle ! " **mur**mured Clitheroe as they entered.

" No—my aunt. Keep shady, **as** aforesaid, and don't get into a cast-iron perspiration."

The room into which they were ushered was lighted only by **the** flicker of a wood fire. At one **side** of this **sat a** tall, thin, elderly lady, screening her eyes from the flame with a palmleaf fan ; at the other **a** somewhat dumpy young woman, who rose as they entered.

" Aunt Henrietta," began Sproat, " I have brought **my** friend, Mr. Clitheroe. Clitheroe, my **aunt**, Mrs. Venable, and **my** cousin, Miss Catherine Venable."

" I am very glad to **see** you, Mr. Clitheroe,"
said the elder lady from her corner. " Excuse
my not rising, please ; I am something of an
invalid."

" Shall I have the lamp lighted ? " asked the
younger. " Can you make out to see anything? Don't stumble over my sewing-chair,
Frank."

" Oh, don't light the lamp !" remonstrated
Clitheroe. " The firelight **is** so much pleas-
anter."

" We think so," said Mrs. Venable. " How
chilly these spring evenings are. Did you walk
all the way out ? "

" No," answered Sproat. **" We** came on a
pair of high-stepping, red-roan steeds. Hist !
Dost not hear them even now snorting at the
portal ? "

" I suppose you are used to his nonsense, Mr.
Clitheroe ? "

" Perfectly, Mrs. Venable."

" You have a widow's fire, aunt," pursued her
nephew. " Permit me to brisk it up a bit with
the bellows. Women never know how to han-
dle a fire."

" If it were not for this fire we should have
perished," rejoined his cousin. " We have been
in this house only a week, Mr. Clitheroe, and
we find everything out of repair, and especially
the furnace. Frank, that stove-man that you
sent out **is a** perfidious wretch. He said the
castings, or something, were cracked, and we
should have **to** have new ones ; and he took

them **away day** before **yesterday and hasn't** appeared since."

" He will return, I know him well—he would not leave me here to die ! " chanted Sproat operatically. " But where's Beatrice **?** "

" You seem to be in good spirits to-night," said **a** voice at the door. " Do you do that often ? "

" Come in, little Treechy, come right **in,**" shouted Sproat. **" Mr.** Clitheroe, Miss Beatrice Venable. Be seated, Beatrice."

The newcomer was far from meriting, in a literal sense, the endearing diminutive which her cousin had applied to her. She was a rather ample young woman, who moved with a certain languid grace, and spoke and laughed in a voice whose deep contralto tones and de- liberate utterance suggested a rich physical en- dowment. Thus much was evident concerning **her,** by the imperfect illumination in the room. As she sat and talked, the firelight shining on her eyes and touching here and there a skein of hair, the salience of her cheek, or the rondure **of** her chin, Clitheroe guessed, rather than saw, that by daylight she would be **a** brown-skinned girl, with tawny hair and eyes of some dark color. She spoke wlth a slight drawl, putting **a** heavy stress on certain words, and with a **sort** of accent which was not definitely foreign, but carried with it tropical, or at least exotic, associations. Clitheroe once asked Sproat if his cousin Beatrice had not lived **at** some time in the East or West Indies.

" Beatrice ? Never," **he** assured him ; but

added, with a laugh, "I don't wonder at your question, though. She *is* sort of sandalwoody and tuberosy."

"Frank has been promising **to** bring you," she said. "You know—or *do* you know?—that we are perfect strangers in Southwick—if you call this Southwick. How many miles is it? Anyway, it was very good of you to come so far to see us."

"**Oh,** it **was very noble** of me," admitted Clitheroe.

"You are a great walker, aren't you?" inquired the other sister. "Frank has told us about your walks together—and about the uncle. We think it's so funny about the uncle."

"What uncle is that?" inquired Sproat innocently.

"Mrs. Venable," cried Clitheroe, "the duplicity of that man is beyond belief. He never let on to me that he had any bloodykin here or anywhere else. He lured me out here in the most unsuspecting frame of mind. He gave our walk this direction as if it was merely accidental. And when he got me as far as the gate he asked me if I didn't think this would be a nice house for the uncle; and then he grabbed me and pulled me in before I could offer any resistance."

All the ladies laughed, and Beatrice said in a tragic tone:

"Mr. Clitheroe, we can never, never be an uncle to you, but we will do our best to be aunties."

At the end of the evening, when they took leave, Mrs. Venable murmured her regrets that they had so long a walk before them at night.

"It's only two miles to the horse cars," said her nephew.

"It seems very long," she replied plaintively.

"That's because it's so long since you walked any, Aunt Henrietta, that you've lost all notion of distances."

"I would offer to put you both up," said Catherine briskly, "but we are all in chaos yet and most of our furniture isn't even unpacked. The next time you bring Mr. Clitheroe, Frank, you must arrange to breakfast with us. I want you to understand, Mr. Clitheroe, that I am the business end of this *ménage*"—and she jingled a bunch of keys in her pocket. "Hear that? Mamma will be your literary aunty and Treech your artistic aunty, and I will be your practical aunty."

When Clitheroe had got Sproat out under the stars he faced him and gazed long and steadily into his eyes. Then they both broke into a violent fit of laughter.

"If you ever put up such a job on me again——" he began.

"What's the matter? Don't you like my cousins?"

"Oh, they are bully cousins, but——"

"I call them rather nice girls—for girls."

"Sproat, they are daisies."

"Oh, come, now, they are well enough. But after all they're not an uncle."

After this the young men's walks commonly tended toward the Wellsville pike and the Venable house. Clitheroe even became a somewhat importunate walker, and Sproat grew, or pretended to grow, a trifle bored by it. One afternoon Clitheroe presented himself at the usual hour at his friend's laboratory.

"Come **on,** you woaded savage; put down that hydrochloric sulphate, or whatever it is; take off your apron, wash your handy-pandies, and let's go and interview Gosh-Darn-It."

"I know what that means," said Sproat as he slowly placed a vial of some orange-colored liquid on the shelves before him and turned around. "Clith, this thing has got to stop. You are getting to be a regular tramp. And you are drinking yourself into the jim-jams on Hiram's root beer."

"Well, are you coming?"

"**No**; go to the aunt, thou sluggard. I can't leave here for two hours yet. I've got some reactions to watch."

"Who said anything about the aunt? I said Hiram."

"Clitheroe"—looking at him steadily—"which one is it?"

"Oh, you be hanged!" said Clitheroe, turning red; and he went out and slammed the door behind him.

Nevertheless, a few evenings after this, the two found themselves once more in Mrs. Venable's parlor. It was June now and Clitheroe had brought a handful of the *Arethusa bulbosa*, which Catherine was arranging in a vase with the spotty leaves of the adder's tongue and a few sprays of mitchella.

"What lovely flowers!" exclaimed Beatrice, coming into the room. "They are orchids, aren't they? Where did you get them?"

"This 'charming little plant in wet bogs, north'—*vide* Gray—grew in Shuttle Pond Meadow, and a mighty wet bog it is. But it's a splendid wild place to be right on the edge of a city, and it's full of fine things. I've no doubt that the otter and the blue heron haunt its recesses, though I've never happened to find them there."

"Oh, how fascinating! Why can't I go there? Is it far?"

"It's a horrid malarial hole," put in Sproat, "a collection of ditches surrounded by pig-pens and slaughter-houses. The corporation ought to drain it. Clitheroe goes wading around in it and trying to persuade himself that it is like the Maremma, or the Pontine marshes, or something. He wants me to go walking there—but there are some things I won't do; I hate stenches."

"Frank hasn't the least imagination," said his cousin. "I wish you'd invite *me* to go walking there, Mr. Clitheroe. What did you call it? Shuttle Meadow? Such an original name!"

"Miss Venable, I shall be proud and happy to introduce you to the wonders of the swamp any day you say. You will appreciate it. It

has character. **Its** name **is** but an index to
its nature."

" Oh, come off !" objected Sproat. " What
has Shuttle got to do with it ? Now if it was
called Pest-house Sink or Frog Hole, or something of the kind——"

" And may I take my sketching things ?
I know there must **be** some delightful bits
there."

"**Miss** Venable, there are a dozen little land-
scapes **in** the meadow, every one of them as
individual as if it was **a** hundred miles away
from the rest. Let me describe you a foreground effect that I noticed just this morning——"

" You may describe it to her, but hanged if
you shall to me," protested Sproat. " I've seen
the place myself, and I won't listen to any stuff
about it. If you go with him, Treech, you'd
better brace up in advance on twelve grains of
quinine and have yourself thoroughly fumigated
when you come home."

It was agreed, nevertheless, that Clitheroe
should call for Miss Venable on the following
afternoon and escort **her to** Shuttle Pond
Meadow. Sproat had arranged to spend the
night at his aunt's and walk into town in the
morning ; and after Clitheroe had taken leave,
he stood at the window, looking out at the dark
and whistling softly. Catherine had left the
room and Beatrice had taken up **a** piece of
sewing and was stitching slowly under the
lamp.

" **A** nice little fellow, Clith," he ventured at length.

She made no reply.

" **But** he will *phantasiren*," he pursued.

"Isn't he a little—ladylike?" She spoke with a lingering inflection, bending low over her sewing.

" I shouldn't call him effeminate."

"Would you call him feminine?"

" Well, he may have a dash of the *ewig weibliche*, perhaps. But what would you call him, now?" facing about from the window.

" He is excitable, but he is awfully sweet."

" What an adjective!"

" You wouldn't like to be **called** that, would you?"

"Not by a woman that I cared for."

" Well, you are wrong. It's what a woman likes best in a man."

"Is sweetness **a** masculine attribute? I thought women liked a man to be masculine."

" Yes, under some circumstances. Oh, you can't understand—you are not a woman."

" Well, anyway, Clith is a nice little fellow."

Shuttle Pond Meadow proved to be very much as Sproat had described it; but also, to **the** eye of sentiment, something as Clitheroe **had** described it. It was a bit of unreclaimed swamp, of perhaps two hundred acres, on the limits of the town. There were soap-factories and slaughter-houses on one side of it, which used its sluggish waters for their drainage, and where the mysterious process known as "render-

ing " annoyed the air. One or two mean little
streets abutted upon another side of it, their
shabby houses, mainly negro cabins, turning
toward it their back yards, a row of sloping
gravel heaps with tumble-down henneries and
rank thickets of burdock and stramonium. A
sandy road gave access to the penetralia of the
swamp, where, on a sort of island fringed with
pollard willows, a German family cultivated a
miniature truck-farm and defied malaria in an
old house littered about with pigsties and
wagon-sheds and the remains of an ancient
apple orchard. The original Shuttle Pond had
mostly percolated away, but the place was full
of stagnant ditches and pools of black bog
water greened over with frog-spittle and all
manner of iridescent scum. Clitheroe apolo-
gized for these unlovely aspects, but Miss Venable was in a gracious mood and made light of
them. She was bent upon the discovery of the
picturesque, and it was not long before she
found it.

Somewhere beyond the ancient orchard they
came upon a plank, bridging a kind of fosse or
moat through which a clear stream ran over
gravel. Crossing this, they found themselves
in a little green meadow, flat and square as a
table top. The willows, alders, button-bushes,
and other fluviatile shrubs which edged it, gave
the tiny landscape an isolation of its own. The
spongy ground was covered with the soft tufts
of the sphagnum, or peat moss, and the water
that soaked their shoes was warm as if heated

for the bath. Clitheroe explained that this was the spot where he had found the arethusa, and that later in the summer the white-fringed orchis would abound among the moss. He sought out a dry, firm area in the middle of the meadow and here his companion, with many exclamations of delight, selected a point of view and got ready her sketching materials. The only building in sight was the old farm-house, a gable of which peeped through the orchard boughs. Clitheroe helped her pitch her easel and adjust the portable camp stool. Then he threw himself down on the grass and watched her spread out her paper and select her pencils.

"Is it permitted to talk to the man at the wheel?" he asked.

"Yes, you may talk all you want, but please don't look over my shoulder. It makes me nervous."

"I can't imagine you being nervous. Still, I'll control my curiosity till your picture is finished."

"It may not be finished to-day; there is so much detail."

"Good; then we'll have to come again."

"That would be lovely, but it may not be necessary. I usually fill in detail from memory, or invent it."

"So that it won't do me any good to delay you by frivolous talk, in hopes of another sitting?"

"Not in the least; besides, it doesn't delay me to talk to me."

She drew at first rather slowly, pausing often, and keeping up her share of the conversation. But presently she grew absorbed, working with swift touches, and her answers became laconic and finally irrelevant. So he ceased talking and **lay** regarding her. She took various graceful poses, sometimes poising the pencil before her face, sometimes leaning backward or sideways **to** examine her sketch from a different vantage ground. Subtle and altogether charming changes **of** expression flitted across her face. Now her eyes were raised and fixed **on** the scene that she was transferring to her paper, now they drooped to the easel. Her brows contracted thoughtfully, then relaxed, and her lips parted.

After a short time she seemed to grow conscious of the intentness of his gaze. She stole sidelong glances at him, her touches grew hesitating, she moved uneasily in her seat, a pretty confusion troubled her features, and once or twice she flushed slightly.

" This is very slow for you," she said at last.

" It's regular lotus eating," he answered, jumping up; " but I see you can't work with people looking on."

" Haven't you got a cigar or something *pour passer le temps?* Or perhaps you could find me another bunch of arethusa."

" I'm afraid it's out **of** bloom ; but I'll tell you what : do you like cress ? "

" What's cress ? "

" Water-cress."

" That peppery stuff that they garnish mutton chops with? No, I can't say that I do. But mamma dotes on it. Does it grow wild?"

" The wildest sort! There used to be a ditch here somewhere that was full of it. Shall I relieve you of my hated presence for a few minutes and go look for some?"

" Do, like a good man."

So he wandered off and botanized about for an hour or so, returning at intervals to ask after the progress of the sketch and to deposit some floral prize or other at the sketcher's feet. By and by he found the cress, and called out:

" Here's stacks of it!"

It was growing in a trench of clear, deepish water, rooting itself in the sandy bottom under the opposite bank. He threw himself down on the edge of the meadow and reached out for it, tearing it away by handfuls and nibbling the pungent leaves. Before long Miss Venable heard him utter an exclamation of dismay.

" What is the matter?" she cried.

" I've dropped my glasses in the water," he returned, "and I can't find them again."

" You poor thing! Shall I come and help you?"

" Oh, no. Go on with your drawing. The water is a little roily, but it will settle soon and then I can see the bottom."

A few minutes passed.

" Found them yet?" she called.

" Not yet," he shouted back. "It's like a blind man looking for his eyes."

"I *will* come and help you," she laughed. "Why, there they are"—as she arrived upon the spot and pointed with her pencil. "Don't you see them? There, near the little clump of weeds."

"I'm afraid I don't," he answered, peering into the stream. "You've no idea how awfully near-sighted I am. Sproat says I smell at a book instead of reading it."

"I'll get them for you," she said, kneeling down upon the brink.

"No, don't. Let them go. They are out of your reach, and you'll wet your dress."

"Will I, though?" she replied. She unbuttoned the sleeve of her blouse at the wrist and rolled it up to the shoulder; then, lying at full length on the bank, thrust her arm into the water and fished up the missing glasses.

"Here, take them," she said, scrambling to her feet; "you may be thankful they're not broken."

"Thankful doesn't begin to express my feelings. But really you oughtn't to have done it. I'm afraid you have wet your sleeve after all."

She stood holding out her bare arm horizontally and, with her other hand, drew aside her skirt to keep it from being dripped on.

"Will you lend me your handkerchief, Mr. Clitheroe?"

"Allow me," he rejoined, and, stepping to her side, began to mop the glistening member softly with his handkerchief. She glanced at him sharply and made a motion as if to withdraw it, but thought better of it and held it still. The water-drops stood on it like beads of dew on marble. His eye took note of one string of them, which tapered down symmetrically from the bigness of a pea to the smallness of a pin's head. The naked limb troubled him with its whiteness and the silky fineness of the skin. As his fingers touched the firm flesh, they trembled with the excitement of a sudden lawless impulse to close upon it, to caress its curves, to carry it to his lips.

"There!" he said abruptly, conscious that she was watching him demurely, and abashed at his own secret temerity; and stepping backward, he thrust the handkerchief into his pocket. She lowered her arm and slowly drew down the sleeve, saying nothing, but smiling an almost imperceptible smile. *Ce sourire si fin—si fin—* what did it express? A shade of irony, perhaps, or even of disappointment, of disdain? What does a girl expect of a man? A respect so delicate that it never forgets the lady in the woman; or a passion so imperious that it does quite the contrary? He was teased by a doubt whether he had gained or lost in her favor by his resistance to an impulse which she must have read in his eyes.

"Mercy!" exclaimed Miss Venable, consulting a watch of the size of a silver dollar, which she drew from her belt, "it's long after six and we must go. But I must do a few strokes more on that willow bush—that is, if you can wait."

"Till doomsday," he answered.

It was growing dusk when they gathered up the drawing implements and bunches of cress and wild flowers and started homeward. They came out of the meadows and turned down the squalid little cross street which led **to** the boulevard. In front of a liquor saloon, where the gas was not yet lighted, lounged a group of "corner-boys," ill-looking thugs with sallow faces, bullet heads, big red ears, and blue mustaches. They were making the summer twilight hideous with curses.

"Tough of **the** evening—horrible tough!" murmured Clitheroe to himself.

As Miss Venable and her escort drew near, the group fell silent and stared at the pair. Clitheroe, too, who had been carrying on an animated conversation, stopped speaking. He felt nervous and quickened his step; but his companion seemed unconscious **of** any reason for haste. She went on talking in a slow, distinct voice and without in the least accelerating her pace. They had hardly passed the door of the saloon when a fusillade of insults assailed them from the rear.

"Get onto de dude wid de chippy."

"Hey, young feller, watcher doin' wid me sister?"

"She aint none o' your sister; she's my best **gal.** Aint ye, Susan?"

A foul jest followed, and a burst of coarse laughter. Even in the lessening light, Clitheroe could see her cheek flush and her eyes sparkle with anger. But she walked slower than ever, as if scorning to retreat, though she had ceased talking.

"Excuse me for subjecting you to this," he said in a low voice. "I think we had better walk as fast as we can." He was shaking with rage and excitement, and he muttered an oath under his breath. "It's the best way never to notice such animals," he added.

"Oh, quite the best way," she replied. There was a tremble in her speech, and it seemed to him as if she fairly sauntered along beside him. At that instant a missile of some sort struck her in the cheek and fell into the bosom of her dress. She stopped with an exclamation, and brushed it off. It was a quid of tobacco. Clitheroe clenched his fists and, facing about, glared furiously through his glasses, then turned and strode on with a feeling of utter helplessness. This show of defiance was greeted with derisive jeers, and their retreat was followed with cat-calls, cock-crows, and shouts of, "Give him a chaw, sissy." "Please dont-cher lick me, Mr. Four-eyes; I aint done noth-ing." "Oh, mamma!" etc.

"I wish," said Miss Venable, coming to a halt for an instant and then marching on again, "I wish Frank—or someone—was here."

Clitheroe winced, as if she had struck him in the face.

"Let me go back and pitch into that gang," he said.

"Not on any account; come on, let's get out of this"—and she began to walk rapidly.

"Sproat would, you think."

"Oh, but he is so big and strong—and so perfectly fearless.   And then," she added, in an awkward endeavor to take the sting out of her involuntary speech, "if there were two of you, they wouldn't have dared."

They went swiftly on and were soon out of reach **of** further annoyance. Not much was spoken **between** them for a while, and when their talk set back to indifferent topics, it was **with** some constraint and manifest labor that it was kept going. Clitheroe had got a hurt in his self-respect, and was smarting with a sense of unmerited shame.   It had been one of those junctures where the carefully spun fictions of civilization are **torn** aside and the brutal facts of human nature stand out in their nakedness : the demand of the female upon the male for protection ; her instinctive choice—her absolute need—of strength and physical prowess.   It was a glimpse into primitive conditions, where the woman falls to the strongest ; a vision of pastures where bulls fight for sleek heifers, and the victor takes the spoils.   In some way he had been unequal to the occasion and she had made him feel it.   And yet what could he have done?   Or what could Sproat have done, or any gentleman or man, unless, indeed, a professional bruiser, or a policeman with billy and revolver?   Should he have involved a lady in a street brawl?   Should he have asked her to walk on, and have gone back himself to get satisfaction from a gang of hoodlums, with the sure result of being shockingly bullied, beaten, perhaps killed? Killing, he told himself proudly, he would not greatly mind. He would have gone to his death for **the girl at his side in** any decent and gentlemanly way—in battle or wreck or fire. **But** an altercation with corner-rowdies, possibly the police court next morning —with Miss Venable on the witness-stand—and the newspapers, and the ironical condolences of his friends—no, the exigency did not seem to call for heroism precisely. What **is** courage **?** Is it not often an accidental mastery **of** the situation? **Or** even, sometimes, nothing more than obtuseness to ridicule?

When Clitheroe left his charge at her door that evening, he knew **that** the bud of promise which had shyly put forth between them would never unfold. There was no definite change in **her** manner toward **him** thenceforth; and when they met again, as they continued often to do, she was as gracious as ever. But there was a subtle readjustment in their mutual attitude. Tried in her balances—coarse ones, he felt—he had been found wanting; **and** she had mortified the pride of his manliness. No man ever really forgives a woman for thinking him **a coward.**

Many times the scene was re-enacted in his dreams with fantastic variations. **He** heard himself say to his companion : "Excuse me for a minute; go on to the end **of the** block, and I will join you **there.**" **He felt** himself, with a sense of exultation and **power,** striking right **and** left among **his** insulters. Then **curiously** the point of view shifted and he saw the whole scene with the eyes of **a** spectator. There was a scuffle ; someone called out, " Cut the d—d jay! " **A** man fell to the sidewalk and lay still. A moment's pause, and then the gang scattered and **fled.** A scream sounded through his sleep, and the girl turned and ran back. In the empty street and the fast-gathering dusk, she knelt down by the fallen man **and** wrung her hands, while his voice pronounced with difficulty the word *Beatrice.*

Awaking from such a dream, Clitheroe would wonder whether melodrama is any more essentially tragical than farce.

II.

A MIDWINTER NIGHT'S DREAM.

A MIDWINTER NIGHT'S DREAM.

THERE was coasting on Rood's Hill. Ever since **four** o'clock, when the schools had let out, the homeward-**bound** farmer, as he reached the top of the opposite ridge, where the cutting wind **made** him draw his old buffalo tighter about his legs, had halted his sleigh for a moment to watch the white slope over against him swarming with little dark objects that moved swiftly down and slowly **up.** Now it was dusk, and the hill was invisible except as a black mass against the western heaven. But still the continuous rattle of the sleds down the steep incline was heard, spreading into a long roar as they neared the bottom, and echoing down the narrow valley to left and right. But when the lamp-posts in the suburban streets began to show their parallel or radiating lines of yellow sparks, and the keen wintry glitter of the stars responded from the sky, the hill became deserted **of all** but a few late lingerers. **Now** the school children were entering their house doors, bringing in with them a rush of cold air. With fingers numb and red under their wet mittens, they were taking off their rubber boots half full of snow, and hanging their worsted tippets on the

hooks in the entry, while the soft lamplight
and the smell of oysters and buttered toast
came pleasantly to their sharpened senses
through the door of the warm supper room.

A few of the bigger boys returned to the
hill for an hour more of coasting after supper,
and did penance later for this prolonged enjoy-
ment, with sleepy eyes and fingers, over the
slates which had to be filled with sums before
they could go to bed. The Gully Brook ran
through a culvert under the hill, and some of
the coasters were dragging tubs full of water
on their sleds up the almost precipitous sides,
and pouring it over the road, worn bare in
spots, to form a coating of ice. The wind had
gone down at sunset, and the air, though in-
tensely cold, was so still that the chill was
hardly felt by anyone in active motion.

About eight o'clock, when the schoolboys'
" pig-stickers " had mostly disappeared from the
slide, **a** new party arrived and took noisy possession. This consisted of young men and
women, equipped with sleds of a substantial
size, convenient for coasting in pairs. Soon the
frosty quiet of the night was broken with feminine talk and laughter, the calling and shouting
of men's voices, and now and then merry
screams where some heavily laden sledge ran
off the track and, gently lifting its starboard
runner, dumped its freight pell-mell into the
powdery snow by the roadside. The double
ripper, the toboggan, and the bob-sled of **a**
more modern era slept as yet " in the bosom of

their causes"; but a plank fastened to two sleds, fore and aft, and steered by a helmsman with a quick eye and an adequate pair of boots, carried some dozen souls and made a sufficient ripper for the nonce.

It happened that, among the groups constantly descending and reascending, two couples reached the top at the same moment. The first pair were walking side by side, the young man carrying the sled by its rope slung over his shoulder. The second lady was seated on her sled; her swain had dragged her up the hill and was panting slightly from the exertion.

"Is that the way you spoil your girl?" said the first man as he gained the starting point and faced about. "You shouldn't do it, Wilmot; you'll demoralize the others. There'll be a strike as soon as they get onto the scheme."

"Well, now," answered Wilmot, "what do you do to your girl to make her walk up?"

"*Make* me walk up, indeed!" said that, young woman, with a toss of her fur-lined hood. "I *choose* to walk up. John Brainard," she cried, with a tragic gesture toward the landscape in general, "wouldn't you be delighted to draw me up that hill if I asked you to?"

"Mr. Brainard," called out the occupant of the other sled almost in the same breath, "aren't you ashamed to put such notions into Harvey's head? He has been perfectly docile till this minute, and he just *loves* to draw me."

"Brainard, let's swap girls," said Wilmot.

At this proposal there were shrieks and exclamations of, "We won't be swapped! As if
we were horses! Yes, or things!"

"How much does yours weigh?" inquired
Brainard, pondering the offer.

"How much do you weigh, Sue?" asked
Wilmot, turning to his partner.

"Never mind," replied the lady addressed,
rising nimbly from the sled. "If I am too
heavy for you, and Carrie wants the pleasure of
walking up-hill with you instead of with Mr.
Brainard, I guess Mr. Brainard can pull me up-
hill once or twice without hurting himself."

"Come along, then, Miss Gillespie," said
Wilmot, twitching his empty sled into position.

"Oh, *I* don't care," said Miss Gillespie, moving slowly away from her first cavalier in Wilmot's direction.

The exchange was laughingly effected, and
Brainard, having seen his new partner comfortably seated, with her feet planted on the cross-
bar, her knees drawn up to her chin, and her
skirts tucked closely around her, gave a short
run, shoving the sled before him, jumped on
behind, and away they sped down the slide.
The long plank "cruiser" was just making up
its load for a fresh trip, amid a profusion of
giggling and chatter, and Wilmot and Miss
Gillespie waited to see it launched and to follow down in its wake. When Brainard's sled
reached the bottom of the hill and came to a
stop his companion sprang to her feet.

"What! Aren't you going to let me draw

you back?" he asked. "I thought that was part of my contract."

"No, indeed," she answered with spirit. "Harvey proposed the swap and I took him up on it, and I'm not going to have you suffer by the bargain. Come along." And she started vigorously up the hill.

"But," insisted Brainard as he walked after her, "you are a borrowed article, Miss Chantry, and borrowed articles must be used with care and returned in good condition. Besides, you are not accustomed to walking up-hill, you know. Wilmot has pampered you into effeminacy by a long course of injudicious indulgence."

"The idea!" she retorted. "I guess my legs are as good as Carrie Gillespie's, up-hill or down"—and her laugh rang out hardily on the crisp night air.

"So, then, I shan't have a chance to find out how much you weigh, after all?"

"Not unless I faint and you have to carry me. But I'll bet anything that she makes Harvey Wilmot draw *her*. I would, if I were she. Now you just see."

And sure enough, on their second flight down the hill, they passed Wilmot dragging his fair burden upward.

"How do you like the exchange?" he yelled after them.

"Oh, lovely—first rate," they shrieked back in concert; but only an inarticulate jumble of syllables reached Wilmot's ear, broken by the rush of the air and the rumble of the sled.

This time Miss Chantry did not rise when the sled stopped. They had run off the track a little way and, reaching out her hand, she broke a piece from the clean snow crust and nibbled it pensively while she sat looking at the stars.

"Confess that that climb has tired you," said Brainard as he stood holding the sled rope.

"I'm **not** the least tired," she replied, "but **the** stopping of the sled gives me a kind of **drowsy** feeling, like ' letting the old cat die ' in a swing. The runners begin to go slower—and slower—and slower, and finally they come to a standstill so softly——"

Her voice died away with a diminuendo effect to indicate the gradual cessation of the motion.

"I hate to shake off the sensation by standing up," she added.

"Don't shake it off, then," he said. "Sit still, and I'll draw you up. Or what do you say to trying the other hill? The grade is not so steep, and I can pull you up it on a run."

"Very well," she acquiesced, "but don't run. You'll break my repose."

A few of the party, deserting the main coast, now somewhat crowded with sleds, had betaken themselves to the opposite rise, which was longer, though of gentler slope. These were presumably sentimental couples who found here a sort of side show or withdrawing room whose comparative seclusion offered a better opportunity for flirtation.

"Shall we try that again?" asked Brainard

of his companion, when they had accomplished their descent and paused in the intervale, "or shall **we go back** to the first slide and **see if** our old pards have got tired of each other and want to swap back?"

"Oh, let's try the new one once more," she answered. "It isn't so swift, and doesn't take my breath away so. Besides, **it's so** nice and retired; it **seems** like going out on the piazza at a dance and getting away from the fiddles and gaslight. But you shan't drag me up **again,** you poor beast **of** burden. 'Seared is, **of** course, my heart,' but hard though I may seem, **I am** not quite adamant. Sometimes I am almost human."

"Well," replied Brainard, "we'll compromise, then, by your taking my arm."

"It's not at **all** necessary," she said, but she took it notwithstanding, and they walked rather slowly up the hill. At times her breathing was a little short, and now and then, where the footing was slippery or rough, her slender figure swayed against him for support; and as they neared **the** hill-top, he even fancied a certain caressing tone in her voice, and something relaxed and confiding **in** the pressure **of** her arm. On the way up they passed two **or** three sleds going down, but they found the head of the slide deserted. By day the eminence where they stood commanded an extensive prospect **of** hill and valley toward **the east.** But under **the stars** all **that** could be seen was a dim white stretch of rolling country broken by mysterious shadows, and sown here and there with the lights of suburban dwellings and of scattered farmhouses beyond. Into this uncertain landscape, whose loneliness and peace contrasted with the noisy mirth that they had left, the pair gazed for a few moments in silence.

" What a lovely night it is ! " said the girl at length.

"**Yes,**" he replied, " it's a sin to go to bed on such **a** night. It's a waste of life. Did you ever try staying up all night out of doors ? " he resumed after a pause.

" No, indeed," she answered, with a slight laugh ; " I am too much of a sleepy head."

" I have often meant," he pursued in a tone of reverie, " to take a whole night some time, and spend **it** *à la belle étoile.* Just think how **much** we miss ! I would like to walk around in the edges of woods and old pastures till the moon set, and watch the changes of the shadows, and listen to the crickets, and hear the sounds of creatures that are abroad in the dark ; perhaps see unknown stars that never rise till after midnight.**"**

" Yes, in summer," she admitted, " it might be nice and wild."

" Or in winter either," he persisted. " Wouldn't it be fine *now,* for instance—this very night—to go on and on, ' over the hills and far away,' and see what strange country we would come to ? "

" Yes," she answered, " if the night would only last forever—but it won't."

" Doesn't it seem **to you,**" he went on, pointing to the east, **" as** if some new world **lay** over
there, all full **of** promise **and** adventure, **if** we
only had the pluck to undertake it **?** It does to
me."

" 'What shall **I see if** I ever go over the
mountains high ? ' " she repeated dreamily.

" Shall we go down this next hill ? " he **pro-**
posed abruptly, after **another pause.**

" What for ? "

" I don't know, but let's."

" Would you **?** "

' ' Wouldn't you ? "

She turned her eyes full upon his **in** the clear
starlight and deliberated in silence :

> The swan's-down feather
> That stands upon the swell at the full of tide,
> And neither way inclines.

At last she answered, " Why, **if** you like."

" Well," he said, and she seated herself **re-**
signedly on **the** sled.

At the bottom of the hill they arose together.
Nothing was said, **but,** as if by **a** common un-
derstanding, they continued to walk on mechanically in the same direction. This time he did
not offer her his arm, and they mounted the
acclivity together without speaking. Once only
she stopped and asked :

" Aren't we getting rather far away from the
others ? "

" We can go back **any minute,**" he rejoined,
and they walked **on.**

At the top of this hill they stopped again. They were now cut off by the intervening ridge from the sounds of the coasting party. The cold had moderated greatly within an hour, and yet there was no film of vapor in the heavens. **It** was one of those halcyon nights, not infrequent in the winter climate of New England—whose changeableness is its glory as well as its danger—when the wind has fallen, and the temperature has risen so rapidly that, in contrast with the previous rigor of the season, the weather has almost a summer balm, and **one** can walk abroad comfortably without an overcoat. In the morning there would be a thaw, but now the absence of the sun kept things still at freezing point. The air was **just** cold enough to be bracing, but so dry and still that it made upon the face only that feeling of freshness which comes with the evening breeze in June.

"**Did** you **ever** read Hawthorne's story of 'Wakefield?'" asked Brainard.

"I don't remember it. What was it about?"

"**A** steady-going old fellow, who has lived a life as regular as clockwork for years with his steady-going wife. All of a sudden an impulse takes him. He goes out one October evening, rents lodgings in the next street, disguises himself completely, and for twenty years never goes home again and is given up for dead."

"Yes, I think I have read it," she murmured.

"Didn't you ever feel that impulse: to cut yourself off suddenly from the past by one irrevocable act ; to burn all your ships behind you ; to step across a narrow crack which you know will widen into a crevice, **and** then **into a** chasm that you can never get back across ? "

" Yes," she answered with a suppressed excitement in her voice ; " I have come to such places and felt the temptation just to put **my** foot across and see what would happen. I have heard something say **in my** ear, ' Now is your chance—now—now ; do it—do **it.**' And then," she added, " I have looked down into the crevice and found no bottom to it, and turned around and gone home again."

" Yes," said Brainard, " we always *do* go **back. We** never have spirit enough to take the venture. I used to ramble along the docks **in** New York and look at the ocean steamers getting ready to weigh anchor, and a dozen times I've been on the point of walking aboard one **of** them and taking passage to whatever part **of** the world it was bound for. But I never did."

She drew a long breath, but answered nothing. And now a tender white radiance began to suffuse the eastern heaven, and presently **a** point and then a rim of silver lifted itself above the horizon.

" The moon ! " they exclaimed together. They watched the planet until its gibbous disk had risen free of the sky-line, and long shadows from trees and fences wavered toward them across the snow crust, sparkling with crystal reflections.

" Sue," said Brainard **in a** low voice that

thrilled with emotion, " shall we go on toward that ?"

" Why not ?" she replied.

As they faced each other in the new light of the moon, it might have seemed that the superstition which attributes madness to lunar influence was not altogether fancy. Whether because his eyes were dazzled and full of moonshine, her own looked larger and brighter to him than by day, and her face had an exalted and bewitched expression. Whatever was trivial or familiar in the girl that he had known **was** strained away, and he found himself alone in the enchanted night with a woman grown suddenly sweet and strange.

" Because," he said, speaking with momentous slowness, " if you dare to go on any **far**ther with me, we may never come back."

" I never take a dare," she answered defiantly.

" Dare you kiss me, then ?" he asked, approaching her.

She made no reply, but in the steady, audacious fixure of her regard he found an answer, and seizing her in his arms, he kissed her repeatedly on her cold cheeks and her warm lips, until she covered her face with her hands and stood as if dazed.

" Now we *have* crossed the chasm," she said when he released her.

" We can still go back," he answered, overtaken with an instant misgiving, as the spirit of the inevitable, which he had so rashly conjured up, rose before him in its full stature.

" What ! after that ? "

" After what ? "

" After what you have done to me."

" Pshaw ! A kiss ! What's that ? "

" Do you want to go back ? " she asked, with an intonation of irony which provoked him into a feeling of shame for his weakness.

" Can you think it ? " he demanded. " No. Get on the sled."

Again she seated herself upon the odd vehicle of their flight, and taking his place behind her, he steered to the east. It needs not to say what relations with others these two had formed or inherited in the world which they were leaving behind them in this unexpected and, as it were, accidental manner. Doubtless in the sober daytime, the ties that they were sundering, the responsibilities that they were throwing off, the places that they were leaving empty forever, would have worn the air of blessings rather than of burdens or constraints. But the solitary quiet of the winter night, that lay all unbroken about them, seemed to shut them away in a universe of their own : an unreal universe of starshine and snow, where all manner of fantastic dreams might come true ; a lawless, unpeopled universe—or peopled by themselves alone, and owing no allegiance to the claims of day.

It was, at all events, characteristic of human nature that, the step once taken, they dismissed all thought of consequences and yielded themselves to the current. As they receded farther

and farther from home, the elastic air and **the**
sorcery of the moonlight, the very unheard-of
wildness of their adventure, raised their spirits
to a mood of buoyant and reckless gayety.
They coasted down all the hills.   Up the slopes
and along the levels, by turns they walked or
Brainard drew her on the sled.   An unwonted
strength and lightness possessed him, and he
felt **no** fatigue ; sometimes they danced or
waved their arms to see the grotesque motions
of their shadows on the snow.   Sometimes they
sang together or whooped in the still air, and
listened for the echo that came back to them
from a hillside or from some old barn standing
alone among the white fields.   For they had
now cleared the suburbs and come out into the
open country.   They talked about themselves
and about the appearances of the night and the
landscape, and repeated fragments of poetry,
and told each other their likes and dislikes.
They avoided all mention of yesterday and to-
morrow, and spoke only of the present.   Their
breach with the past was complete, and they
seemed to themselves to be wandering on and
on in a dream from which they would never
awake.   The girl's bearing toward her new-
found lover was as capricious as the circumstances in which they found themselves.   At
times she suffered his caresses and even returned
them ; and then again, with an abrupt alterna-
tion of coyness, she would say, " Please let go
my hand, Mr. Brainard, and walk farther off."

The moon rose higher, a little wind began to

blow, and puffs of powdery snow were whirled along the road and across **the** fields. Miss Chantry had not spoken for nearly an hour, and had remained sitting on the sled while Brainard drew her over a long plain. Of a sudden she asked, " What time is it ? "

He looked at his watch, turning the face toward the moon.

" My watch has stopped," he answered. " I forgot **to** wind **it** yesterday, and it has run down. But I know that it must be long past midnight."

" How far have we come ? "

" Oh, five or six miles, I should say."

" Is it too late to go back ? "

" To go back ! " he exclaimed. " You can't mean it, darling "—and he came and knelt beside her in the snow.

" It *is* too late," she cried passionately, pushing him away. " They have missed me long since ; there is a hue and cry after me now. Oh, what a fool I am, what a fool ! " and she burst into tears.

" Don't, sweetheart, don't," he remonstrated ; " you will never repent it, I promise you—I promise you."

But he felt a sinking of the heart, and a sickening uncertainty of everything. The reaction had come to them both, and the awakening.

" Where are you taking me to ? " she inquired at length.

" I hadn't thought distinctly of that—or of anything else **but** you. **But** Reddingham is about five or six miles ahead, and Clark's Mills **is** still nearer. We can go there."

"So that **is** your 'new world,'" she exclaimed bitterly. "Reddingham, and Clark's Mills!"

"There **are** places beyond Reddingham," he said sullenly. "It's on the railroad, and we **can take** the morning train to—I don't care where—the uttermost parts of the earth, if you **like.**"

"The morning train—the morning train!' she repeated. "There should be no morning for fools like us."

"Sue," **he** entreated, "be brave. You are tired, you are excited. You'll feel better soon."

"I *am* tired," she answered listlessly, "and I am cold."

"Of course you are, poor love—poor love, and I am a brute **not** to have thought of it. See here, I've got my brandy flask in my overcoat pocket ; take a pull at this and it will warm you up."

She took a draught of the dark-brown liquor, in which the moon made golden reflections, then shuddered, and settled herself once more on the sled.

"We could go back," said Brainard hesitatingly, "if you insist upon it, but—good Heavens, to what ? And it's as near to Reddingham as to Burlington."

"No," she said, shaking her head vehemently. "We're in for it. Go on. But you are tired. Let **me** walk."

" Not I—not I ; keep your seat. Do you feel warmer now ? "

" Yes, but awfully sleepy."

" Lie down on the sled ; it's long enough ; I'll put my coat over you, and perhaps you can get a nap."

She curled up on the sled, with her hand under her head. He took off his heavy overcoat, tucked it around her, and cutting off a length of superfluous rope from the sled, wound it about her twice and tied it.

" Now you are tied on, like Mazeppa," he said, with a forced laugh.

" You need the coat," she murmured.

" Not in the least ; it hampers me dreadfully. You shut your little eyes now, and I'll take you to Reddingham in no time."

Grasping the rope, he toiled on with renewed energy. At first he felt chilly without his overcoat, but the exercise soon warmed his blood. Gradually he was overcome by drowsiness. The vast white landscape glimmered and swam before his eyes. He caught himself nodding, but still staggered mechanically forward, though with increasing slowness. About cockcrow they passed through a little town, and he thought of Sir Galahad :

> When, on my goodly charger borne,
>   Through dreaming towns I go,
> The cock crows ere the Christmas morn,
>   The streets are dumb with snow.

This was Clark's Mills, a compact manufac-

turing hamlet about three miles from Reddingham.   The houses stood up stark and dead in
the moon.   In one window a light was burning,
and Brainard thought, as he pushed the sled
rapidly before him down the pavement, how
strange it must sound to the citizen, waking
casually in the night, to hear the rumble of runners, as **if some** ghostly sledding party was dis-
porting itself in silence at that uncanny hour in
the deserted street.

After leaving the town, the hills grew steeper
and the scenery wilder, intersected from left to
right by valleys which narrowed into woody
ravines.   From the depth of these came, now
and then, the long howl of a farmer's dog bay-
ing the moon, and once the yell of a screech-
owl resounded from a distant wood.

Miss Chantry seemed to have fallen asleep.
The impression of unreality, the sensation of
moving through a dream, grew stronger in
Brainard's mind.   All manner of wild and fantastic images flitted through his brain; his eyes
got heavier and heavier.   Nothing kept him
from falling but the exertion necessary to drag
the sled through the snow.   For the track had
become now almost unbroken : he had evidently left the highway and was on some un-
frequented road where few sleighs had passed.
At the top of a hill he roused himself and came
to a halt.   He was dead tired and felt really
unable to go **on.**   The moon was now getting
low in the west.   It must be, he thought,
about three o'clock, and they ought to be near-

ing Reddingham, but no symptom of a town appeared. The summit was a high one and overlooked a region of snowy hillsides topped with gray woods. He stepped to the sled and gazed down upon the unconscious girl. Her finely chiseled features, in the moonlight and in the relaxation of sleep, had the softness of a child's. Her long lashes shadowed her cheek, whose polished roundness, as it took the light, looked almost infantile or cherubic, while beneath the curve of her under lip lay a little well of shade. There was something helpless and confiding in her attitude. She lay on the sledge like a bride in her bride-bed, with a suggestion of domestic intimacy which brought into Brainard's heart a sudden rush of pity. The stopping of the sled aroused her.

"I am not asleep," she said, opening her eyes, but not offering to move. "Is anything the matter?"

"I am afraid we are lost," he replied.

"Lost!" she exclaimed.

She sat up at once, and then, removing the coat which had covered her and freeing herself from the rope, she rose to her feet and stared about her.

"Yes," said Brainard wearily, sitting down on a rock which projected from the snow; "Reddingham ought to be over there somewhere, and not more than a mile or two away. But I see no signs of it. I must have taken the wrong turning after leaving Clark's Mills."

"Can't we ask our way at some house?"

" We haven't passed a house for over an hour
and we seem to be getting into a more and
more God-forsaken country.   This road is taper-
ing out, for one thing, and we will have to go
back or else take to the crust."

He was still speaking when, on the opposite
hillside, a ruddy glare flashed out on the pale
night—a parallelogram of living coal, against
which could be clearly descried the black
figure of a man moving forward and back.

" What **is** that ? " cried Miss Chantry,
startled.

" Ah," he exclaimed, leaping to his feet, " it's
a charcoal pit.   Now I know about where we
are.   But we have come up into the Woodridge
hills, a long way off from the direct road to
Reddingham."

" Hadn't we better go there and inquire our
way ? " she suggested.

" I suppose **we** had," he replied after a
moment's hesitation.   " These charcoal-burners
are apt to be a tough crowd.   But there seems
to be no other way.   It looks like the mouth of
hell," he added, " with Satan feeding the fires."

They watched the weird spectacle for a few
minutes without moving.   It was only one
more fantastic vision of this night of fantasies
and dreams.

From the open door of the pit, a path of rosy
light streamed down the hillside and across the
frozen surface of a small pond in the hollow.
The illumination also made visible a group of
two or three buildings which stood a little to

one side of the pit and somewhat **lower on the** slope.

" The shortest way will be to leave the road here and **go 'cross lots** over the crust. It will bear," said Brainard, stamping on a sample piece of it to try its strength. " Come on, quick, before they shut off the light."

He took up the sled and helped her over **the** ditch and the rail fence into an open hillside pasture. For the last time they took their seats upon the sled, and **the** runners were soon gliding swiftly **down the** glazed surface of the field, which glinted in the moonbeams like the icing of a gigantic pound-cake. They descended **at** a constantly accelerating, and **at** last really frightful, speed. Brainard had all that he could do **to** guide the sled by digging with his heel into the crust. Miss Chantry gripped the **edges of** the board and held on with suspended pulse, while the air **rushed past** their faces like **a whirlwind.**

" Pray Heaven there are no stumps or fence-posts in the way," was his secret thought. But in a few seconds, to his great relief, they reached the bottom and rushed out upon the snow-covered ice of the pond. Suddenly the girl screamed. Right across their course, **and** only a few yards ahead, she saw a black streak of open water. She had just time **to** throw herself sideways upon **the** ice, falling close to **the** edge **of** the water, into **which** the sled, **and** Brainard with it, plunged and disappeared. **At** the same moment the door of the coal **pit** closed and the light went out. Instantly she began shouting for help, but it seemed an age before an answering hallo came back from the hill, and a still longer age before Brainard's head emerged from the belt of dark water, rippling under the moon, upon which her eyes were staring in an agony of fear. He rose near the opposite side of the opening and grasped the edge, which was even and firm, having been cut with an ice plow.

"O God! O God!" she cried, wringing her hands, "what can I do? I can't get near you."

"Go back from the edge," he gasped; "I can hold on. Call for help."

"I have. Oh, please hold on. Only a minute. There! I hear them coming."

Steps were now heard crashing hurriedly down the hillside through the crust from the direction of the charcoal pits.

"This way!" she called. "For God's sake, be quick; there's a man drowning. Oh, Fred, can you hold on a bit longer?"

"Yes," he answered, with chattering teeth, "but the cold is horrible. Look out for a board."

She ran to and fro distractedly, but not even a stick was to be seen on the white floor of the pond. But now a man ran out from the opposite bank and approached the opening.

"Hang on," he called out. "The ice is solid; it won't break. I'll get you out in a jiffy."

He neared the edge cautiously and, lying

down at full length, held out **both** hands to Brainard.

"Leave go the ice and get a grip on my hands," he directed.

"Oh, how can I help?" cried Miss Chantry. "Where can I get a board or something?"

"I **don't** want no board," returned the man; "run around **to** this side, quick, and lend a hand."

The opening was only a **few** rods long, and in a twinkling she was beside the prone form of the rescuer.

"Now, lady," said the latter, "you git down **on** your knees, take a holt o' this arm, and pull. Brace yourself agin the ice—it'll hold. I'll yank on the other arm. When we git you up's fur's the waist, young feller, you jest lay your leg out on the ice and **we'll** roll you out."

There was a short, sharp struggle, and **then** Brainard **lay** shivering and dripping on the ice.

"You had a close call this time, boss, and no mistake," said the man, who was panting from his exertions. "How in hell did you git here, anyway?" **he** added with open-mouthed wonder.

"Never **mind** that now," rejoined Brainard, rising with some difficulty to his feet; "I must get to **a** fire **and** have these clothes off in **a** hurry. I'm chilled to the marrow."

"Do you **feel** stiff? Can you run? Well, then, cut up **to** the shanty. There's a fire and there's clothes, sich as they be, and there's whisky."

The three ascended the hill and the **man**
threw open the door of an unplastered wooden
cabin, divided by a rude partition into two
rooms. In one of these was an air-tight stove
which threw out an intense heat from **a** fire of
oak billets. In the other was a bed, and a row
of coarse garments hung from the wall. Miss
Chantry, who was pale, silent, and very much
agitated, paced the floor nervously in the outer
room, while their host took Brainard into the
penetralia, helped him to strip off his wet cloth-
ing, and furnished him with a change of raiment.
In a few minutes he joined her by the fire and
assured her that he was as good as new. The
charcoal burner went out to look for the sled.

"Well, now, what next?" inquired Brainard
as the companion of his adventure paused opposite him in her restless walk. She looked at
him with a new resolution in her eyes.

"It was not **to** be," she said. "This is a
providence—an interposition."

"Oh, no," he returned, "it is an interruption,
that is all."

"Just think," she whispered, "if you had
been drowned." She shuddered, and covered
her face with her hands.

"Oh, come, now, Sue," he remonstrated, and
tried to take her hand.

"No, don't," she cried, breaking away; "I'll
never forgive myself. I've been dreaming all
night. I've been—I don't know what I've been.
But I'm wide awake enough now."

He was silent,

" What time is it?" she asked.

He pointed to a small wooden clock that stood on a shelf.

"Four o'clock!" she exclaimed. "There is just one chance for me. If I can catch an early train I can get home, perhaps, before they are up. I have my latch-key, and I'll say that I left Harvey to see Carrie home, and came back early from the hill with you, and let myself in and went right upstairs to bed. There's just that chance—that one chance—that no one sat up for me at home, and that I haven't been missed. Quick, where's the man? Maybe he has a horse and sleigh, and can take me over."

" Sue," began Brainard, again approaching her.

" No, no," she broke in vehemently. " You can't turn me—you can't talk me out of it. You know that I'm right. Don't you?" she asked, looking at him searchingly.

" And so our little melodrama ends in a farce," he said, evading a direct reply to her appeal. " It's always so."

" It is better so," she answered.

" You can't expect *me* to say yes to that."

At this moment the charcoal-burner entered. He had been unable to find the sled, and explained that it had probably sunk to the bottom of the pond owing to the weight of the iron on the runners.

" Have you got a horse and sleigh?" inquired Miss Chantry hurriedly. " Could you take me over to the depot at Reddingham in time to

catch the first train west ?   **Do** you know what
time it goes ? "

" Why, cert, lady," answered the man slowly ;
" I've **got** a horse and cutter, and kin hitch up
and take you there easy. It ain't but three
miles, and the train leaves at 4.55."

" It will get you to Burlington before half-
past five," added Brainard.

" But ain't you goin' to have some breakfast
with me 'fore you go, ma'am—or leastwise a
cup of coffee to warm you up? I ain't no
slouch **at** making coffee."

" No, no," she **said** beseechingly. " Please
—please take me at once, and don't let me miss
the train."

" *All* right, ma'am," he responded good-
naturedly, and taking down a lantern, went outside, where they heard him presently opening
the stable door and getting out the horse.

" I shall have to ask a favor of you, Mr.
Brainard," she said, blushing slightly. " I
haven't my purse with me—the ticket—the
man———"

" Why, am I not going with you ? " he asked.

" No, no ; it won't do for us to be seen together at the station. You must stay here, and
go back later."

" But I don't like to let you go alone."

" It is perfectly safe," she answered ; and he
handed her his purse and was silent.

" What, ain't the gentleman going too? "
inquired Brainard's deliverer, as Miss Chantry
was helped into the cutter and bade her cava-

lier good-by. "There's lots of room for three."

"No, cap, I'm going to stay here till my clothes get dry, and keep house for you till you get back."

"Wal, I'll be gosh darned!" remarked the puzzled driver, as he gathered up the reins. "Say, mister, when you git sleepy you kin turn in in the bed. I've got a shake down for myself, and you'll find a pipe and tobacco on the shelf and a jug of whisky in the locker, near the bed."

"Mind you catch the train," Brainard called after him.

"You bet," came back on the wind, and horse and sleigh disappeared under the setting moon.

Brainard slept profoundly, and it was deep in the day when he awoke. At first he lay still and stared at the wall. He could not remember where he was, but an unaccountable feeling of relief possessed him. His eyes were fastened idly upon an object on the wall which he could not at once identify. It was nothing but a big knot in the rough planking of the cabin, through which the sun streamed, making a kernel or focus of light; but it looked like a great rose or ruby, glowing with vivid scarlets and crimsons, and burning with an intensity which flooded his eyes and his whole being with radiance, and seemed an emblem of some inward happiness. Slowly the twilight between sleep and waking cleared into full consciousness, and the memory of the night's adventures came back to him. But still he lay in a kind of blissful trance, thinking of the chasm in his life from the brink of which his feet had gone back ; of the bonds and the duties and the habits that had seemed, in the witching light of the moon, a load to be lightly cast off forever, but which now, in the healthy sunshine of the new day, became infinitely sweet and sacred. He heard the drip, drip of thawing snow from the eaves. He heard the charcoal-burner whistling outside, and presently the steady blows of his ax.

After a while he rose and, finding his dry clothes by the stove, dressed and went outdoors. His host was chopping down a tree, one of the last of an army whose stumps projected here and there from the snow, and whose trunks had been converted into charcoal.

" Hello, colonel," he called out, suspending his labor, " you ain't up, be you ? I swanny but you have slept solid. Guess you was out late last night, wasn't you ? I put some breakfast by for you to keep hot, but, gosh ! it must be all dried up by this time."

" Thank you, I'll go in and help myself to a bite. Did you make the train ? "

" Wal, we did, and ten minutes to spare "— and he resumed his work.

Brainard's sense took note of the odor of fresh chips with a keen pleasure. The sun, many hours high, poured a dazzling light over the white, undulating country. A few chippy-birds were hopping around the doorstep and their cheeping made music in his heart, as did the tinkling sound of little rills of snow-water dissolved in the thaw and stealing off downhill under the crust. The broad, commonplace face of day cheered him with a conviction of the good health of the world, and a thankfulness that the place in that world which he had come so near forfeiting was still kept open to him.

At Reddingham Station and on the train he was lucky enough to meet no acquaintances. But as he was making his way from the depot at Burlington to the main street, he encountered Wilmot, who greeted him with:

" Well, well! What became of you and Sue last night? We looked for you all over the hill and couldn't find even a mitten of you."

"Why, you don't expect people to coast all night, do you? Miss Chantry got cold and tired, and wanted to go home."

"Did she seem to be a trifle miffed, too?" asked Wilmot, with a slight shade of anxiety.

" Why, no. What should she be miffed about?"

"Well, what should Miss Gillespie be miffed about? All the same, she was. She wanted to go home, and when I looked around for you, and you were gone, and I told her I guessed she'd have to accept the escort of yours truly, she tossed her head and said, you and Sue appeared to like the all-hands-change-partners figure so well that you seemed inclined to keep it up for the rest of the dance."

"Oh, **no**!" said Brainard, with an uneasy laugh. "**It** answered well enough for an evening, but it wouldn't do for good."

"Thank you. Same here. But girls don't take a joke worth **a** cent, and **I** think I'll go around **to** Sue's and make **my** peace. She might have been miffed and you not seen it. Men are so damned obtuse, you know."

Miss Chantry was punctual at breakfast that morning, and was rallied by the family on her paleness.

"**Coasting doesn't** agree with everyone," said her **brother Gilbert**; "makes some people sea-sick."

"You must have got home very late," said her mother. "**I** didn't hear you come in."

"On the contrary," she asserted, "it was very early."

"Well," said **her** father, from the window, where he stood **in** his slippers, newspaper in hand, and regarded the street, "it's the last of **the** coasting, for the present. The January thaw has set **in** and the wind is dead south."

III.

A COMEDY OF ERRORS.

A COMEDY OF ERRORS.

MR. WILLIAM MERRIMAN, JR., described by his friends as a rising young lawyer, came uptown one evening in December about an hour later than usual. It was his habit to stop somewhere on the way up and dine in a leisurely way, and then to get to his room at half-past seven or thereabouts. On this particular evening, however, he had lingered over his coffee and newspaper, and now, as he reached the door of his apartment, he was made aware of the lateness of the hour by the roar of the grate inside. The chambermaid had been instructed to leave the blower up when she kindled the fire, by which means the reluctant draught was coaxed into efficiency just at the time of his customary arrival. It had now an hour's extra headway, but the faithful domestic, with the unreasoning obedience of a Casabianca, stuck to the letter of her instructions. Accordingly, when Merriman entered the room he found things booming. A loud smell of varnish went up from the legs of the chairs, a crimson glare from the bottom of the grate smote upon the carpet, and a fiery crack defined the outline of the dull red blower.

This last being taken down, the walls and **ceil-**ing bloomed like a rose ; and while the glow-ing iron snapped **and** cracked, **as** it slowly cooled, Merriman got himself into dressing gown and slippers, lighted a big pipe, settled himself **in his** easy-chair and, by the steady firelight, proceeded **to** read a brace of letters which he had found on his mantel.   The first of these ran as follows :

BLANKSKILL-ON-HUDSON,
December 18, 187-.

DEAR **MR.** MERRIMAN :

Mamma is ill with a cold, so I am doing her cor-respondence.   We came up to Blankskill very un-expectedly, but now that we have opened the house we mean to spend Christmas here, and we have hit on quite a bright idea.   We are going to ask about a hundred people up **for** the evening of Christmas Day and have that little comedy over again which had such **a** success at the charity entertainment— " If She **be** not Fair for Me,"—you know.   We shall expect you **to** take the same part you had before. The actors ought **to be** here by the 23d to re-hearse, if possible.   So you must R. S. V. P.   We shall keep *a few choice spirits* through the holi-days, and of course mamma says you are to con-sider yourself included in that list.   There will be sleighing, and, I *hope*, ice boating, if the river only keeps frozen.   So you must make arrangements to leave your anxious clients for a few days.   We will let you go back in time for New Year's calls.

Very truly,
HARRIET VAN SHUYSTER.

The other letter bore the postmark of a small hill-town in Berkshire, Mass., and these were its contents, to wit:

CHUCKATUCK, December 18, 187-.

MY DEAR COUNSELOR:

Can't you get off at Christmas for a week up here? We are alone, as usual, my sister and myself, and can't offer you anything brilliant in the way of entertainment. You used to like to take long walks in college and then come home and " chin" over a wood fire. We can do that here to satiety. We can take you sleighing too, if the snow doesn't drift off the roads. Then you needn't go to church and hear me preach if you don't want to. I will lend you the MS. of my sermon, which will do just as well. Say you will come.

Yours faithfully,

CHARLES HOPKINSON.

P. S.—You take the Housatonic Railroad at Bridgeport and stage for Chuckatuck at Whistle-ville. Fishing through the ice on the pond.

The warmth of the room had a relaxing effect on the will, and the recipient of these invitations sat a long time in a luxury of in-decision. A complacent smile stole now and then across his face, and his thoughts were evidently as rosy as the clouds that curled upward from his meerschaum.

Presently footsteps came along the hall, fol-lowed by a smart rap at the door.

"Come in," called out Merriman lazily, not troubling himself to look around.

The door opened, and a tall, Mephistophelian-looking man, with a sallow face and black mustache, stepped into the room. "For God's sake!" he exclaimed; "do you keep a Turkish bath here?"

"Hallo, Willett; **that** you? Come in. Why haven't you been in before?"

"**In** before! Who do you think is coming into **such** a hell on earth? Open a window, quick."

"Why, **of** course," laughed Merriman. "I was thinking of it, **but** I couldn't get up the energy. Just open that one in the alcove, and then come and sit down."

Willett flung up a window, and then, approaching the mantel, said, "Give me **a** pipe. I've got time for just one smoke."

"You're always in **a** hurry," grumbled his friend. "*Sans aucune affaire et toujours affairé*—that's you. If you want a big-Injun smoke there's old Popocatepetl on the table. If you want **a** little smoke for **a** cent you'd better take Spitfire there on the shelf."

Willett picked up a pipe and began filling it from a large jar representing the face of the sleeping Holofernes. "Which it is limited," **he** said, looking around the small room; but added approvingly, "which it is a *bijou.*"

"It *is* kind of decorative. But haven't you been here since I took these quarters?"

"Never. You used to be on the other side of the shebang, one flight up, last time I was here."

"Well, how **are** you, anyway? **To-night** you come *gerade wie gewünscht :* **I** want your professional advice. Sit down, **and I'll** put the **case.** Have some whisky first?"

"I will always have some whisky—if properly approached."

"Then read those two letters while I make **a tod,** and tell me what to do."

Willett took **the** letters and read them gravely, through. He frowned **a** little **and** drew down his heavy eyebrows, sucking **silen**tly at **his pipe, as** he read.

"Well **?**" **said** Merriman at length. "What does the calumet say to my brother **the** saga-more? Here, take your firewater and give **us** your talk."

"Which do you want to do?"

"**I** can't make up my mind."

"Toss up a cent."

"**At** least, **I** know what **I** want to **do,** but **I** don't know what I ought **to do.**"

"In that case do the one you want to do."

"Willett, you have no Moral Earnestness. **I** have long suspected it : now I know it."

"Oh, yes, I have, lots of M. E.; **but** where does it come in here?"

"*Die Sache ist nämlich die :* Hopkinson is always asking me up there, and I've never been. I don't want him to think that I'm cutting him. Hopkinson **is a very** good fellow, if he *is* **a** parson, **and we** were **very** thick in college— chummed together for a year, in fact. I'm un-**der** considerable obligations to him in one way

and another. I ought to go. I really ought."
Merriman repeated this with the futile emphasis
of irresolute persons when they are trying to
bully themselves into a determination. As he
sat in the light of the fire, his face offered a
strong contrast to the swarthy, sardonic countenance of his friend, its length of jaw and high
cheek bones. Merriman's face, with its deli-
cately cut features, pale complexion, and straw-
colored side whiskers, expressed lively intelli-
gence combined with a certain weakness. " I
know it will be a beastly bore," he continued :
" muffin-worries, and calls from parishioners;
introduced to the senior deacon and the village
belle—with ringlets—and the man who keeps
the academy, probably a graduate of Podunk
University. And then the sister is doubtless
the worst sort of old frump. The fact is, I am
sorry for Hopkinson. He has the making of a
man in him, but he is stuck off there on a
huckleberry hill with a salary of twelve hundred
dollars, and he's getting into the narrowest kind
of rut. I suppose he reads nothing but the
Missionary Herald and that sort of thing.
Last time I saw him he looked all gone to seed."
Merriman paused to contemplate the mental
image of the Rev. Mr. Hopkinson, and sipped
meditatively at his glass.

" The Van Shuysters are swellness?" suggested Willett.

" Rather swell—rather swell," answered
Merriman complacently. " I wish they wouldn't
put a crest on their note-paper; and ' Blankskill-

on-Hudson' is too much agony. But women will do such things."

"And the Miss V., I suppose, is prettier than a spotted purp?"

"Well, she's not bad. But you've seen her, haven't you?"

"No, I think not. Oh, you'd better take them up and have a good time of it. If you go to Hopkinson's, now, you'll get nothing but grocery cider with your Christmas dinner, and have to go out on 'the stoop' for a smoke. Whereas if you do the other party, you can 'travel with great drinking, deliciously money spend,' like your French friend—wasn't it?—who wrote you that letter from Montreal."

"Yes," said Hopkinson, laughing at the recollection: "'deliciously money spend'—that was the phrase."

"Then on Sunday you'll have to hear—out of common politeness—two sermons at least from your host; whereas at Blankskill-on-Hudson, I infer, they knock spots out of the Christian Sabbath."

"Willett, I fear you are little better than one of the wicked."

Willett eyed him severely for a moment, and then replied, "Far be it from me to speak slightingly of your religious opportunities. I am myself—since my engagement—a polished corner of the temple. Go, by all means. Go up, Baldhead. Yes, go up to—Hardscrabble, was the name?—and my blessing go with you."

"But you haven't told me what excuse **to give** Hopkinson."

"Tell him you had accepted the other bid before you got his."

The two young men regarded each other steadfastly and then burst into a simultaneous explosion of laughter.

"**You are** a bad man—a bold, bad man," **said** Merriman. "**Have** another tod, and fill **up your** pipe."

"No; I must **be** going," replied Willett, looking at his watch. **He** rose and wandered round the room, examining the various articles of "bigotry and virtue," and then, with an abrupt "Good-night," took his departure.

Coming in like the monitions of the worldly voice in "Dipsychus," Willett's counsel had fixed for a moment the vacillating impulses in Merriman's mind; and, while the impression **was** fresh, he lighted the gas and dashed off answers to his two invitations, sealed and addressed them, and sent out for a messenger boy to post them.

Let us follow them to their destinations.

Mrs. Van Shuyster and her daughter were sitting by an open fire in the library of their country house at Blankskill-on-Hudson. The wind shook the French windows, which opened on a wide piazza. Thence the eye ranged over a lawn glittering with crusted snow, over clumps of Scotch firs weighed down with piles of feathery white, over the ice-bound river far below and the dreary opposite hills. The driveway which wound across the lawn **was well** broken with sleigh **tracks, but** just at present no living thing **was** in sight except a few men stirring about **the** big ice-houses on the other bank. **The** elder of the two **ladies** was a comely matron, with the long Dutch nose and heavy Knickerbocker chin. **The** same features were repeated in Miss Van Shuyster, but with the softer emphasis of youth. She had, too, her mother's **fresh** complexion and tendency to stoutness. Mrs. Van Shuyster **was** busy **over** some mysterious piece **of** needlework; **her** daughter was listlessly turning over the pages of **a** novel. Now and then the latter yawned and looked dreamily **out** upon the winter landscape. A young-lady cousin **lay** asleep **on** the **sofa, and** her breathing was more than audible.

" How that child does sleep ! " said Mrs. Van Shuyster softly.

" How that child does snore ! " rejoined her daughter.

" I'm afraid she has taken **a** bad cold."

" **Of course** she has—going out last evening without the ghost of an overshoe. She's too giddy for any use."

" Isn't it almost time for the mail ? " asked Mrs. Van Shuyster after a long silence.

" Yes, **it** is—after time ; and there's John now."

And in **fact** the jingle **of** sleigh-bells was heard, and a cutter came up the drive. The elder lady went placidly on with her work, but the younger threw down her book and stepped to the window.   The slight noise aroused the sleeper, who sat up under her rug and rubbed her eyes. " Have I been asleep ? " she asked.

Both ladies laughed, and Mrs. Van Shuyster answered, " Well, you sounded like it."

" Oh, **did** I snore — *did* I snore ? How horrid ! Why didn't you wake me up ? "

" Call it ' stertorous breathing,' Charlie," said Miss Van Shuyster soothingly.

" Call it ' fiddlesticks ' ! You'd have let me do it all the same if the room had been full of men." She approached **the** mirror over the mantel and gazed ruefully at her reflection. " What a nose I've got on me ! " she continued. " It's a regular purple. I know I shall be a perfect fright next Tuesday. I'm mad enough to go upstairs and bite the bureau."

" Go up, instead, and put some cold cream on your nose," suggested her cousin.

" It will go down before Tuesday," said her aunt, inspecting the offending member with the **air** of **a** connoisseur.

" Oh, *do* you think so ? "

" It won't if you fuss with it," said Miss Van Shuyster brutally.   " Put some cream on it, and let it alone."

At this point the door opened, and a servant brought in some letters, which she handed to Miss Van Shuyster, who tore them open eagerly, one after another, and announced the contents : " This one is from the Hoffman Duyks ; they are all coming ; that's good. H'm ! Mr. Lampick sends regrets; he has to go to Washington. Well, somebody else will have to take *Alonzo*. Fortunately the part is short; but then his mustache is a great loss. Here's a note from Mrs. Madison May. *He* is coming, but *she* can't. Well, no one wants *her*. Oh, here is one from Mr. Merriman. It is to you, mamma: will you read it?"

"Why, no, my dear. I suppose they are all to me, aren't they?"

"Oh, *is* Mr. Merriman coming?" broke in the impetuous Charlie. "I think he is just too lovely! *Don't* tell me that he isn't coming! It would darken all my young life." She clasped her hands with a tragic gesture and lifted her eyes appealingly to her cousin, who colored slightly under her gaze.

Miss Charlotte Middlesex—known to her intimates, who were numerous, as "Charlie"— was a rapid brunette, with a baby face and large, innocent eyes. She had also a low, cooing voice; and under cover of all these advantages she managed to say and do the riskiest things with an air of confiding simplicity.

"There must be some mistake: I don't understand," began Miss Van Shuyster, glancing over the letter. "The envelope is addressed to mamma, but the letter begins, 'Dear Charlie.'"

"Why, it must be for me!" exclaimed Miss Middlesex.

"Do be still, you ridiculous girl! Mamma, see if you can make it out."

Mrs. Van Shuyster took the letter and read it out, as follows :

DEAR CHARLIE :

It would give me the greatest pleasure to **take** up your offer for the holidays, but I have just written accepting **a** bid to make one at a Christmas party at Mrs. Van Shuyster's, **up** the North River. I'm very sorry, but it **can**'t be helped. Perhaps I can run **up** and see you **some** time before long and take **in the** walks and the fishing through the ice. Don't fail to let **me** know when **you** come down to New **York.** **Please** give my **respects** to your sister, and believe **me**

Yours faithfully,

WILLIAM MERRIMAN.

"Oh, now I see it all," said Miss Van Shuyster. "He was writing to us and to some other people, and he has exchanged envelopes. What a thing for a *man* to do! And he always laughing at us for being Mrs Nicklebys and sending bundles by kindness of **Mr.** So-and-So, instead of by express, and for being afraid to write on postal cards for fear the post-office men would read **it.** Oh, we'll never let him hear the last of it. Don't lose that letter, mother, for the world. We'll learn it by heart and quote it to him. We'll make his life perfectly *meeserable.*"

"Hattie!" said her mother warningly. And then, looking at the letter again, "**It** seems that we may expect him, at any rate : he says as much to his correspondent here. Put the letter

in my desk, **dear, and I will give it to him** when
he comes. It would hardly be **worth while** to
send it back, I suppose. He will start before it
can reach New York."

"I wish I knew who got the other letter, and
what was in **it**," murmured Miss Middlesex.
" It might **be** something awfully compromising.
Wouldn't it be fun **if** it was ?—like things **in**
Shakspere, you know."

"Compromising **to whom ?**" demanded her
cousin sharply.

" Oh, **not** to you, dear, not to you, of course ;
but maybe to ' Dear Charlie,' whoever he is.
Charlie—Charlie **!** **It's** quite **a** coincidence,
isn't it ? "

"I don't see any coincidence about it," **an**-
swered Miss Van Shuyster.

Meanwhile the other letter had reached port.

The postmaster—who was likewise the store-
keeper—at Chuckatuck had pigeonholed the
last newspaper of the afternoon mail. The few
people in waiting had taken their departure,
but the ring of village loafers still hugged the
stove, on whose red-hot sides the sizzle of the
frying tobacco-juice acted as a gentle stimulant
to conversation. The talk was suspended
for a few minutes by the entrance of a young
lady wrapped **in** a hooded cloak with scarlet
lining, who brought in with her a breath of cold
air. The gossips eyed her with the respectful
and furtive curiosity due **to** the minister's sister,
while she called for her mail, received a single
letter, and went quickly out again. Inside, the

stream of debate resumed its deliberate course.
Outside, **the** wind was sharp and the twilight
gathering. As the minister's sister turned into
the slender path trodden in the snow, which led
down through the pasture, across the frozen
brook, and up the hill to the parsonage, she
noticed that the lamp had already been lighted
in the study and was sending its glimmer
through the network of bare orchard boughs.
But her impatience to see the inside of the letter
was such that she opened it as she walked
along, and spelled out its contents by the fad-
ing light. The envelope was directed to the
Rev. Charles Hopkinson, though in opening it
she was not committing one of those small
feminine breaches of honor over which the cynical reader might naturally " chortle." The
Rev. Charles, in fact, had gone off for a day or
two to a " convocation "—a mysterious period-
ical ceremony whose recurrences formed the
only dissipations of his quiet life. He had
commissioned his sister to open all his letters
in his absence. Some of them might need immediate attention. In particular, he was expecting an answer to his invitation to Merriman.
If the latter was coming, there were certain
household preparations to be made, of which
Miss Hopkinson should have timely warning.
On the other hand, if he was not coming, she
was free to accept an invitation to spend Christmas with some friends at a distance. She had
resigned herself to the self-denial of staying at
home to help entertain her brother's old college

chum, and her resignation had been made easier, perhaps, by a certain flutter of expectation natural to a youthful spinster about to be confronted with a rising young lawyer from New York, whose fascinating qualities her brother was never weary of describing. Only a few evenings ago, as they sat before the study fire, Hopkinson had said, breaking out from a long reverie, "Bill Merriman is one of the few fellows that I know who haven't changed for the worse since leaving college. When I go to the city and hunt up my old classmates I come back feeling melancholy. They seem to me to have grown coarse, and I probably seem to them to have grown narrow. They act as if they were glad to see me, and are very kind, and all that, but I can tell from their talk that their ideals have become lower. They've lost their old enthusiasms; they're all for money—money. I've no doubt they think me a stick. Now Merriman has retained a kind of fine boyishness: he is just the same old chap, and it makes me feel younger to see him." Miss Hopkinson made no reply to this outburst, and presently he went on: "I'm afraid, though, from what he told me the last time I saw him, that he is going too much into society. A young lawyer had better stick to his books pretty closely at first."

"But think how society would suffer," suggested his sister.

"Oh, come, now, don't be ironical. I see you are bound to nurse a prejudice against Merriman."

" Well, if he is such a swell as you say, what
are we going to do to entertain him up here?
Shall we take him to the meeting of the Dorcas
Society, or show him the public buildings?
There's the jail, now, and the bank. Or he
might go to the store and be weighed."

"Oh, you don't know Merriman; he likes
this sort of thing just as much as you or I."

" What sort of thing ? "

" Well—nature, for instance : walks, etc.
He will be interested in your collection of
ferns."

" How kind of him ! "

" And sitting by the fire this way. We used
to have many an owl over the fire Saturday
nights in old South Middle. And that reminds
me : I must get that box of hickory nuts down
from the garret. I hope they haven't turned
rancid. And there's some of the canned cider
left that Deacon Appleseed sent in at the dona-
tion party. But, Sarah dear, I've told you a
dozen times that you must not give up your
visit on our account. Emma and I can run the
house well enough and take care of him without you."

Sarah's answer to this was to rise and come
behind her brother's chair. She took hold of
both his ears, and, bending over, kissed him
on the forehead. " You dear old thing ! " she
said. " You and Emma run the house ! I
think I see you ! What would you get to eat ?
No ; if he is coming I shall stay, though I know
I shan't like him."

"Yes, you will," asserted her brother warmly : "he always makes himself agreeable to women. The only thing about him that you may not like at first is his—not exactly frivolity; Merriman is not a frivolous man at bottom—but I am afraid he is getting some worldly notions in New York. I mean to have a serious talk with him, if I get a chance."

It may admit of a doubt whether Merriman's worldliness was really a very strong objection to him in Miss Hopkinson's mind, or whether, in her secret thought, she cherished so strong an assurance that she should dislike him as she pretended. She chose to take a defiant tone in speaking about him to her brother; but who knows what little plans she made for the time of his visit, what little touches of newness her simple wardrobe privately underwent, what innocent dreams lent a subdued excitement to her maiden meditations ?

And now the epistle was come which would decide her plans for the holidays.

A single quick glance, as she took it from the hands of the postmaster, had told her that the postmark was New York and that the handwriting was—well, was similar, in fact, to the autograph under a certain photo in the Rev. Charles Hopkinson's class album.

Miss Hopkinson was not conscious what a charming "spot of color" she added to the demi-gray landscape as she walked slowly on, intent on deciphering the letter, or now and then stood still to make out a word. The snow

creaked under her sauntering footsteps; the
wind, which made a wintry music among the
dry stalks of golden rod along the path, swayed
her light figure, and blowing aside her cloak,
exposed the scarlet lining.   It also rumpled the
fringe of yellow **hair** that hung down under the
eaves of her hood, and when at last she finished
the letter and lifted her indignant eyes, the
darkening heaven which they encountered was
less deeply and softly blue.   Indignant eyes,
for they had just read the following words :

DEAR MRS. VAN SHUYSTER :
   Your invitation comes just in **time** to save me
from another, which I couldn't very well have
declined, to spend my Christmas with a clerical classmate who "keeps a few sheep in the wilderness,"
with an old-maid sister for shepherdess.   Accept my
gratitude, and expect me on the 23d to rehearse,
though I think I remember the part well enough.
                    Yours thankfully,
                         WILLIAM MERRIMAN.

   The snarl of emotions which filled the young
lady's breast, the reader will hardly expect me
to untangle.   She gave a fierce little laugh and
clutched the wicked missive tightly as she
strode up the hill.   Had she been given to
soliloquy—a habit convenient to novelists, but
seldom, alas! indulged in in this work-a-day
world—her monologue might perhaps have run
in this wise : "Well, you *have* given yourself
away, Mr. William Merriman!   So I'm an old
maid, am I, and a shepherdess, and Charlie is

a 'clerical classmate'? — poor Charlie, that thinks he is his best friend, and all the while he is laughing at him behind his back and sneering about us to his rich acquaintances like Hattie Van Shuyster. (What a queer coincidence that he should be going to the Van Shuysters'! Of course he can't know that Hattie is a friend of mine.) He thinks we are not 'swell' enough for him. I always knew he would prove to be a snob, a perfidious, ungrateful, odious snob," etc., etc.

The letter raised a number of problems, which she puzzled over as she sat at tea that evening. Ought she, for instance, to destroy the note, or keep it till Charlie came back, and then show it to him and let him return it to Merriman without further comment than to mark on the envelope, in lead-pencil, " Opened by mistake by C. H." ? This latter plan would have a fine crushing effect. But then she knew that the letter would make Charlie feel badly, and she was not quite sure that he would approve of her having gone on to read it after seeing that the address was a mistake. Men are so fussy about these little points. Then, again, ought she under the circumstances to give up her projected visit or to spend her Christmas at home? " Charlie will be awfully lonely," she thought, " but then what a chance! what a chance!" And she smiled maliciously as she packed her trunk and put the letter in the tray of it.

The next morning her brother came back.

She greeted him with more effusion than usual, and hung on his arm as he stood warming himself by the air-tight stove in the hall.

"Any letters?" he asked after a while.

"Oh, yes, a few lines from Mr. Merriman. He can't come, because he has made another engagement for the holidays. So I've packed up, and I told Mason to have the stage stop for **me** after dinner. But, Charlie dear, I don't feel at all like going and leaving you alone. Please reconsider and go with me. The Van Shuysters will be so glad. Hattie has been wanting to know you for years; and you know what a point they made of your coming."

"No, no; I can't," answered Charlie. "Jenkins has made arrangements to exchange with Burroughs next Sunday, and couldn't preach for me. Old Mr. Stone may drop off any minute, and the family wouldn't like anyone else to conduct the funeral. I shouldn't probably enjoy the party much anyway, I should have to hurry back so. I'm sorry Merriman can't come, but I shall have a snug Christmas and get that work done for the *Christian Andiron* that I promised to send them a week ago. You didn't burn Merriman's letter, did you?"

"No; I laid it down somewhere. You might find it on the library table—and then, again, you mightn't," she added under her breath, as she ran off to the kitchen for a final interview with Emma, the "help."

The late lamented Van Shuyster had amused

his leisure with scientific and artistic dabblings,
and had built a large room with a skylight
adjoining his library, in which to carry on
experiments in the black arts of photography,
electricity, and molding in clay. This, Mrs.
Van Shuyster, who had a passion for theatricals,
had lately reorganized into a sort of dramatic
saloon, closing the skylight and arranging a
tasteful little stage at the upper end. Here, on
the evening of Christmas day, was seated an
audience of some two hundred guests, waiting
for the play to begin. The room was unlighted
except by the reflection from the drop-curtain,
which hung softly brilliant in the radiance of
the foot-lights. On either side of the stage
were painted in fresco grotesque masks, socks
and buskins, and other histrionic insignia. The
walls were decorated with Christmas greens
and illuminated Gothic texts expressive of senti-
ments appropriate to the season. A subdued
hum of conversation filled the assembly, a faint
perfume hovered on the air, and here and there
a jewel flashed in the dimness. There were
yet some minutes to spare before the curtain
would be rung up, and Merriman, who had
finished dressing for his part, stepped out upon
the stage in the costume of a Spanish alcalde of
the seventeenth century. Finding a crack in
the curtain, he began a leisurely survey of the
audience. He was presently joined by Miss
Van Shuyster, who emerged from a thicket at
L. L. E. in a ravishing peasant costume with
shortish skirts and high heels, and with her

arms, which were shapely but rather massive for a young girl, bare to the shoulder.

"Well, well! Such curiosity!" she exclaimed.

"'Sh!" **he** responded softly; "here's another hole; come and peep."

"Who is here?" she asked. "I haven't **seen a soul** yet outside of the *troupe*, I've been **so busy** getting things ready. Mamma and Charlie have been receiving the people. Aren't you awfully nervous?"

"Frightfully. I know a few of the audience, **but** more of them I don't. The room is rather dark to make out faces. Come and do Helen on the battlements **of** Troy pointing out the leaders of the Greeks to the Trojan old men. I'll be a Trojan old man. Don't I look **venerable** in this dress?"

"Talk about dresses! I never, *never* will be a peasant again. Don't you think it's horrid?"

He turned and inspected her critically. She cast **down** her eyes and stood demurely to **be** looked at, with the least little conscious red on her cheek. "You mean," he said, "that it's a trifle—unsecluded? Well, you can't expect me to object to that."

"*Ach! gehen Sie! gehen Sie!*" she answered, turning away. "Where is that peephole?"

"Here is mine, and there is a larger one for you close by it."

It was in effect so close that, as they stood side by side to play spy on the audience, her

dress brushed slightly against him, and he became aware of that subtle aroma which is
neither the breath of the lips nor the fragrance
of the hair, nor yet any definite odor like violet
or musk, but which is a delicate suggestion and
reminiscence of all these and holds a natural
affinity with silk and kidskin. She stood very
still, as if the proximity was not unpleasant.
Merriman was evidently on easy terms with this
young lady, and it occurred to him now, as it
had often done before, with a certain complac-
ency, that her inclination toward him was
rather thinly disguised. Augustus Montague
had once said to him at a ball—Augustus Montague, whose acuteness of observation was
only equaled by his frankness of speech :

"Damn it, Merriman, why don't you go in
for Miss Van ? I'll bet my sweet life she says
'Yes.' A bonanza, my boy ; millions in it.
Law's awful slow ; you'll never get rich at it.
Fire out your office-boy, and take Miss Van
into partnership. Wedding in Grace Church :
tour out West ; settle down on the old woman
for a few months ; and then Mrs. M. finds that
her throat is delicate and she can't stand this
beastly changeable climate, and so off you go,
up the Nile and everywhere, first bestowing a
life-pension on yours truly in gratitude for this
advice."

"In sooth, Augustus," Merriman had answered, laughing, "I might do worse. And
there she is now ; I'll go ask her—to dance."

"Conceited cuss ! but the women like him,"

murmured Mr. Montague, as he watched his friend making his way up the room.

And indeed Merriman had often acknowledged to himself in his more worldly moods that he might do worse. Wealth, with its refinements and elegancies, had lost none of its glamour in the eyes of an ambitious youth reared in a New England factory town, who had struggled with poverty through school and college and had come to New York with a sharp appetite for success. Besides, Miss Van Shuyster, though somewhat heavy and commonplace, **was not** without personal attractions. Montague's remark passed through his mind again this evening as he stood adjusting his eye to the little slit in the canvas.

The spectators were grouped with **a** picturesque irregularity. There was no slope to the floor of the theater, but the seating had been arranged as far as possible so as to let those at the rear look over the heads of those in front. Nearest to the stage was a double row of men squatted Turkish fashion on the carpet—here and there among them a young woman lifted above the general level upon a cushion or *brioche*. Conspicuous among these was Miss Charlotte Middlesex, chattering and laughing with her admirers. " Now, I want you to understand," she called out, " that we all belong to the *claque* down here, and I shall expect you to back the show."

" Shall **we** applaud everything, Charlie ? " asked one,

"No, indeed. **Oh, I have my** favorites, I **tell you. You must wait for me** to give the signal. When **I** want you to clap, I'll tap Mr. Block on the head—so—with my fan, **and he** will **lead** off. Three taps means an *encore.* Mr. Block, I hope your head isn't *very* soft, for I know **I** shall **get** enthusiastic in the sentimental parts."

"Let me get **you a** camp-chair, Miss Middlesex," cried another ; "you will get awfully tired without a back."

"No, no; I **don't** want a chair; Mrs. Estridge's knees make a lovely back. Pinkie Buchanan, **be** a good fellow and pass me that paper of burnt almonds. **Isn't this** awfully, awfully jolly? Like sitting on the grass at **a** circus!"

Behind this advance guard, led by **Miss** Middlesex, were several rows **of** low wicker settees; behind these, higher tiers of upholstered sofas and chairs ; and, at the rear of the **room,** a few seats mounted on tables. On one of the highest of these, as upon a throne, sat a girl whose face seemed to form the apex of the whole assembly and the focus of all **the** scattered rays of light in the **room.** It was a short, rosy face, crowned with heavy coils of straw-colored hair. **The** mouth was large. The dark eyes were leveled steadily at the drop-scene, and Merriman **had a** nervous feeling as **if they** looked through the canvas **into his own. Her** *ensemble* was so striking that no jewelry would **have been too** rich, **no colors too pronounced,** which she might have chosen to wear. **But** she was dressed very simply in a white cashmere, with a necklace of the palest amber for her sole ornament.

"Who is that very handsome girl at the back of the room?" inquired Merriman, after regarding her fixedly for several minutes.

"Handsome girl?" echoed his hostess. "Which one? Where?"

"Don't you see? In **a** white dress; right in **the center of** the **last row.**"

"Well, to be **sure!** How glad I am she's **come!** Why, it's **Sally** Hopkinson, an old fem. **sem.** chum of mine; and I haven't seen her for a year. Do you think her pretty?"

"Pretty! She is gorgeous."

"She has a lovely complexion and hair. But her mouth is big, and her eyes don't match with the rest **of** her face."

"I like a generous mouth," said Merriman. "What's her name? Hopkinson? Where from?"

"Why, **she** is a compatriot of yours—from Massachusetts. She lives in a little country **town** in Berkshire, with her brother, who is a minister. We used to call her the Puritan maiden Priscilla at the seminary. I'm so glad you like her looks!"

At this moment the prompter's bell rang sharply, a hush fell on the audience, and the curtain began to tremble. Merriman and his companion fled into the side-scenes just in time to avoid an exposure.

The reader shall not be bored by a description of the play which followed, nor of the manner in which the various actors acquitted themselves, nor of the comments of the spectators. Let it pass silently over our stage, like the dumb show in an old comedy, noting only that one of the mimes carried all through his *rôle* a sub-consciousness of a figure in white and a pair of indigo eyes that stared at him from the end of the auditorium. In spite of which distraction, he acted with his usual cleverness, and won loud applause from Charlie Middlesex and her band of *claqueurs*.

When the play was over, the company filed out of the theater and stood about in groups in the large parlors and library, discussing the performance. Merriman, having washed off his war-paint, went in search of Miss Van Shuyster, whom he found receiving congratulations on the success of her theatricals.

"You promised to introduce me to Miss Hopkinson," said Merriman, joining her circle.

"Oh, yes. There she is now, talking with Charlie and Mr. Block, at the end of the room. I haven't spoken to her yet."

The greeting between the two young ladies was effusive.

"You dear little Yankee!" said the hostess, kissing her guest several times in rapid succession. "Why didn't you come sooner? You've got to stay with us, now, till after New Year. And why didn't you bring your brother? I want to introduce an admirer, who says that he

knows your brother and is **so** disappointed that
he didn't come with you. **Mr.** Merriman, Miss
Hopkinson."

Merriman bowed eagerly, and Miss Hopkinson rather coldly.

" If you are Charlie Hopkinson's sister," he
began, **" I feel** as if I knew you already.
Charlie and **I** were chums at college, you know,
for **two** years."

" Yes, I have heard him speak of you," said
Miss Hopkinson, not very emotionally.

Merriman was about to speak again, when
Miss Middlesex broke **in,** fixing her large eyes
on him, sighing and waving her fan slowly :
" Oh, Mr. Merriman, how *beautifully* you
acted ! I don't see how you do it. I never
could. I should break right down."

" Miss Middlesex has too much individuality
for an actress. **She** couldn't lose herself in her
part," said Merriman, laughing.

" No, it isn't that," she replied, shaking her
head mournfully ; "but **I** could not face the
audience—never—*never !* 'Twould be blush,
blush, blush with **me,** like that poor man in
Hardy's novel."

" Oh, we all know how bashful you are, poor
thing !" said Miss Van Shuyster. " What
made Mr. Block run away when we came up ?"

" He's gone to smoke **a** cigarette in the
billiard-room," answered Charlie, pouting. " I
wanted to go awfully, but my stern mamma
has come down on my cigarette-smoking. She
says it stains my finger-tips. Do *you* think it

does, Mr. Merriman?" And she held up a row of ten little rosy puffs.

"It does," said her cousin quickly. "And it burns holes in the front breadth of your dresses."

Miss Hopkinson looked slightly shocked.

The door of the supper-room was now thrown open, and there was a general move in that direction.

"Miss Hopkinson, will you let me get you something to eat?" asked Merriman, offering his arm. She took it, and they walked away.

"I can't abide your prim friend, Hattie," said Miss Middlesex, looking after them. "She always makes me feel vulgar."

"She isn't prim when you know her; at school she was quite a romp—a regular fiend in pillow-fights and such things."

"Let us go into the conservatory," proposed Merriman to his companion : "it's nice and cool in there, and plenty of room."

He seated her on a porcelain garden chair, and she listened to the splash of the little fountain, in whose basin a few goldfish were swimming about, while he went to get her some supper. She occupied this interval in thinking over a plan of campaign, but reached no definite resolution further than to stand on the defensive and be guided by circumstances until the opportunity came to mass her heavy battalions on the enemy's center. Presently he returned with some salad and biscuits, and stood before her, holding her plate, while she arranged the napkin over her lap. " You can't think how surprised I am to meet you here," he said, as he handed her the plate and their eyes met.

" Why ? " she asked.

" Well, I had no idea that you knew the Van Shuysters."

" Hadn't you ? " she answered indifferently. But she thought to herself, " That means as much as, ' I took you for a little country school-marm, with your hair full of hay-seed, and here you are all of a sudden in my own *monde*.'"

" And, besides that—didn't you know ?— Charlie asked me up to Chuckatuck to spend Christmas ; and if it hadn't been for my engagement here I should certainly have been there now."

" Yes, I knew he was expecting you."

" Well, it seems that I did the lucky thing, after all, when I accepted Mrs. Van Shuyster's bid first."

" Oh, I think you did : you would have been awfully bored at Chuckatuck."

" No ; you misunderstand me. I shouldn't have been bored at all. But I should have missed seeing Miss Hopkinson."

" Oh, no ; I was to stay at home if you came, and help entertain you."

" That would have been rough on you, but I don't know but what it would have been nicer for me. I should have had you and Charlie more to myself, you know, than I can here. Come, now, what were you going to do for my entertainment? Methinks I see visions **of** moonlight sleigh-rides, **and** candy-pulls in the kitchen. I should like **to** see you with the housewife's apron **on,** doing the domestic veal for Charlie."

" I *never* wear an apron ; and I hate sleigh-rides and **candy-pu**lls—they freeze **your** feet and blister your hands," returned **his** *vis-à-vis* ungraciously.

There was silence **for a** while as they dispatched their respective salads. Merriman was thinking to himself, " What a queer girl to be Hopkinson's sister ! There's no mistake about her being a smasher ; but she isn't exactly genial." Finally, he recommenced : " **How** is Charlie, anyway ? I haven't seen him **for an** age. Why didn't you bring him with you ? "

" Oh, **he couldn't leave** his sheep alone in the wilderness, you know," she answered, with a resentful **glance.**

Merriman vaguely recollected having **heard** or used this phrase somewhere, but **he** could not place **it** definitely, and **he** was quite at a loss to interpret the look which accompanied it. " Let me get you some oysters," he proposed. "No? Look out for the train of your dress, or it will get **into** that **fountain.** I **never** come into a conservatory without thinking of an adventure I had **at** the Buydamms' party last winter. I took my **partner into the** conservatory to **feed her, and, while she** was explaining to me that one side of **a** begonia-leaf is always bigger than **the** other, I tripped backward over the rim of the fountain—it was a smaller one than this, only held a tureenful—and sat right down in it. I slapped the water all out of the basin, and killed one goldfish."

" How funny!" said Miss Hopkinson, laughing in spite of herself. " What did you do ?"

" My partner had great presence of mind, and fortunately there were few people in the parlors. They'd mostly gone out into the supper-room. She took my arm and covered my retreat nobly as far as the stairs, and I got up into the dressing room, slipped on my overcoat, and made my escape without further disgrace."

" All of which shows how dangerous it is to feed botanical young ladies in a conservatory."

" Ah," began Merriman with a sentimental air, " if botany were the only dangerous thing about them !"

" Well," she broke in hastily, " please don't repeat your sitz-bath on my account. I shouldn't have the same presence of mind, I'm afraid."

" Should you scream ?"

" No; I should laugh."

" How hard-hearted you are! Are you through with your plate? Let me take it away and get you some cream and things." He disappeared, much elated by the thaw in her humor. " She isn't so chilly, after all," he said to himself. " It seems that she does know how to relax and *desipere* a bit *in loco.*" He returned quickly with a plate of ices and a glass of sherry.

"You may keep the sherry, please," she said, as she took the plate.

"Doesn't the dominie let you drink wine?" he asked.

"As if he could stop me if I wanted to!" with a toss of the head.

"Then, if you won't, why, 'Drink to me only with thine eyes.' *Prosit*, Miss Hopkinson." And he raised the glass to his lips. "Do you know," he went on presently, "that I can't get over my surprise at your being Charlie Hopkinson's sister? You look so entirely unlike him. I can see perhaps a slight family resemblance in the shape of the face, but your eyes are totally strange."

She cast down the features alluded to and reddened slightly, moving uneasily in her chair with a look of annoyance. She found herself drifting into a sort of mild flirtation with this offensive young man, whom she had come prepared to dazzle into a sufficient state of admiration and then to snub into abject humility—perhaps by handing him back his letter with a lofty and withering speech of some kind, if a good opportunity offered. But her indignation, which had seemed so virtuous at Chuckatuck, appeared to her now rather overstrained. Perhaps the letter was not so very bad, after all. To be sure, it was a shame for him to write so to anyone about Charlie. But as to the *spretæ injuria formæ* which had unconfessedly formed no small part of its sting, that was atoned for by his evident admiration and astonishment at sight of the "old-maid sister" and "shepherdess" whom he had traduced. Certainly the man was amusing enough, and probably meant well, although he was so very, very light.

"Miss Hopkinson," he now resumed, as he finished his sherry, "what relation is a fellow to his chum's sister?"

"I should say that depended on what relation he was to his chum."

"Oh, first-cousin at least. I think twice as much of your brother as I do of my cousins—whose name is legion. Why doesn't he get a nice little parish near New York, where he wouldn't be so cut off from his old friends?"

"Perhaps he can get along without his old friends as well as some of them seem to without him," she answered with asperity. Her resentment had suddenly come back to her, provoked by the insincerity and the patronizing tone of this last remark.

"I don't quite know what you mean," said Merriman.

As fate would have it, she pulled her handkerchief out of her dress-pocket at this instant, and a letter which was pulled out with it fell on the floor. He stooped to pick it up for her, and, as he did so, she rose, and gathering up the train of her dress, replied, "Perhaps you *will* know what I mean, Mr. Merriman, if you will read over that letter again, which belongs to you, by the way, and not to me. Keep it, please."

As Merriman in blank amazement proceeded

to open the letter and glance over the familiar writing, Miss Van Shuyster, followed by a tall young man, appeared at the conservatory door. " So here is where you two have been hiding all this time ! " she exclaimed. " I've been looking everywhere for you, Sallie, to introduce Mr. Polhemus. Miss Hopkinson, Mr. Polhemus."

The gentleman bowed and said, " They are making up a set in the library, Miss Hopkinson : shall I have the honor ? "

" Certainly," she answered, courtesied slightly to Merriman, and departed on Mr. Polhemus' arm. Miss Van Shuyster remained in the conservatory.

" Since when, Miss Van Shuyster," broke out Merriman excitedly, holding up the letter, " is it considered a delicate joke among young ladies to show each other the correspondence of their gentlemen friends ? "

" I don't understand you."

" Perhaps you may, then, if you will look at this, which is addressed to *you*, but which Miss Hopkinson has just handed to *me*."

She took the letter, and, glancing over it, said immediately, " This letter was never sent to me, but another one was. If you will look at the address on the envelope, I think you will see how Miss Hopkinson came by it. And I assure you I don't feel complimented by your suspicion."

Merriman glared in a bewildered way at the envelope, and then replied, " I beg your pardon ; I see it all now. I'm the jackass of the nineteenth century. But I wish you had told me of my mistake before. It has put me in a very embarrassing position with the Hopkinsons."

"How could I know who your letter was for?" she demanded warmly. "I intended to mention **your** mistake to you and give you back your letter, but it slipped my mind entirely till this minute. If people will be **so** stupid as to mix up their correspondence, they must take the consequences."

"It's all my fault," said he; "but it's very unfortunate."

"**You** seem to care a good deal about Miss Hopkinson's opinion," **she** said, with a tremor **in** her voice.

"Of course I do," he answered.

At this moment the vivacious Miss Middlesex darkened the door, and began, "Oh, Mr. Merriman, I had almost forgot. Such **a** giveaway **on** you! Who—who is 'Charlie'? Why, what's the row?" looking from one to the other.

"'Row' is not **a** lady-like expression," responded Miss Van Shuyster severely; "and I **wish** you wouldn't apply your slang terms to me, please." And with that she swept from the room.

"What *have* you **been** doing to my cousin, Mr. Merriman?" inquired Charlie.

"Oh, nothing, Miss Mildlesex: *amantium iræ*, you know," said Merriman, with a feeble laugh.

"I know that's Latin; but I think you might translate."

"Come, let's go and have a dance," he proposed.

"I think you are *hawrid*," she said, taking his arm; "but I'll get it all out of Hattie. I can make her tell me anything I want by threatening to tickle her if she doesn't."

"Mrs. Van Shuyster," said Merriman, about half an hour later, approaching his hostess, whose matronly figure was filling an armchair in the recess of the library, "I had hoped to accept your invitation to stay a day or two, but I find that a reference which comes on to-morrow will make it absolutely necessary for me to catch the down train to-night."

"Oh, I am sorry! Couldn't you postpone it, or something? One or two of Hattie's friends are to stay through the week, and she had counted on you to beau them about. Hattie," she called out to her daughter, who was talking to a group of ladies near by, "Mr. Merriman says that he has an engagement which will take him to New York to-night."

"We should be very sorry to interfere with any of Mr. Merriman's engagements," returned Hattie.

"Then I will bid you good-evening, ladies," said Merriman.

"Must you really? Well, then, good-by," said Mrs. Van Shuyster, putting out her hand. "We are ever so much obliged to you for coming and for your help in the play, and so sorry that you can't stay."

The younger lady simply bowed, and Merriman withdrew. He went at once into **the** next room, where the dance was just over, and approached Miss Hopkinson, who was standing by **the** mantel-piece, talking with her partner. "May I speak with you **a** moment, Miss Hopkinson?" **he** asked: "I have to catch this **train**."

"Why, I suppose so," she responded, with an **air of** surprise, "**if Mr.** Polhemus will excuse **me**."

"Oh, certainly," **said** Polhemus, glaring at Merriman and moving off reluctantly.

"Miss Hopkinson," began our hero, "may I ask **whether** your brother commissioned you to say anything to me about that unfortunate letter?"

"My brother has not seen it."

"Not seen it! Who then?"

"**I** opened the letter. Charlie was away for a day or two, and he told me to open all his letters, **as** some of them might need answering before **he** got back."

"And you didn't show **it** to him afterward?"

"No; I was afraid it might hurt his feelings: so I merely told him that **you** had made another engagement."

He heaved **a** sigh of relief: "I can't thank you too much for your thoughtfulness. I wouldn't have had Charlie see that letter for anything."

She, too, felt relieved. She had half expected to be put on her defense for reading his

note after she saw that it was meant for someone else. But it did not apparently occur to
him that she had done anything blameworthy.
This magnanimity touched her, as did also
his manifest contrition. Her heart began to
soften.

"Yes," he resumed, "I am glad he didn't
see it; but I am just so much the sorrier that
you *did*. I have made a bad impression on
you, Miss Hopkinson," he said solemnly.

She made no reply, but her eyes danced
mischievously.

"I have just had an awful quarrel about it
with Miss Van," he went on ruefully. "I
seem to have put my foot in it all around."

"I don't see why you should have quarreled
with *her*."

"Neither do I exactly; but I have. But the
worst of it is that you are down on me, too, because I called you an old maid."

"Oh, yes, I'm furious," she laughed.

"Well, now, how was I to know? Where
has Charlie been hiding you away all these
years? Why didn't he ever have you down to
class-days and things? The idea of a man's
chum having such a pret—having a sister, you
know, and never saying anything about it!
From all *he* ever said, you might be a hundred
and thirty-five years old."

"Then you ought to have respected me all
the more."

"Oh, yes, so I should. Reverence for your
gray hairs, and that sort of thing. You ought

to write Charlie's sermons for him.   Come, now,
Miss Hopkinson, you know that if you really
were an old maid I wouldn't care so much for
your opinion—as Miss Van Shuyster twitted
me with doing just now."

"**Say no** more about it, Mr. Merriman.   I
forgive you the 'old maid.'   It didn't matter
anyway."

"But it matters to me that you shouldn't
form an opinion of me from that letter.   The
fact is that when I wrote it I was fresh from a
talk with my cynical friend Willett, who always
puts **me** into the mood for saying all sorts of
reckless things that I don't mean in the least."

"Willett?" murmured Miss Hopkinson.

"Yes; if you knew Barnaby Willett—Mephis-
topheles Willett, we call him—and could hear
him talk for half an hour, you would understand my frame of mind when I dashed off that
confounded note.   **In fact,** if it hadn't been for
his advice, I should have cut this appointment
anyway and followed my impulse to go up to
Chuckatuck.   I wish I had!"

"Mr. Barnaby Willett!   Did *he* advise you
not to go to Chuckatuck?   I wonder why."
Her eyes had suddenly grown big and round,
and her whole attitude expressed a newly
aroused interest.

"What?   You don't know Willett, do you?"

"Oh, yes," she answered, with a little laugh
and a little blush, "very well indeed.   Mr. Willett and I are—I am engaged to be married to
Mr. Willett."   And she looked him straight in

the face, while **her** blush gradually **deepened,** until it forced her **to cast down her** eyes **in be-** witching confusion.

Merriman felt the ground give way from under his feet. His jaw dropped and his eyes goggled wildly. At last he laughed aloud. "So this **is** all a put-up job on me!" **he ex-** claimed.

"'A put-up job?' I **don**'t quite know what that means. **But if** you mean there has been a conspiracy against **you—no,** there hasn't. I **never knew** till this minute that you and Mr. Willett were acquainted. And I am **sure** he has never told me **a** word about you or about your coming up to Chuckatuck."

"Well, the whole thing is simply enough **to** make a man luny," said Merriman. "I talked half an hour to Willett about you and Charlie, and he never let **on,** by word **or look,** that he had ever heard of either **of** you before. And he made all manner of **fun** of country parsons, **etc., and** advised me by all means to take up the **Van** Shuysters' bid and give Chuckatuck the go-by. What *was* his game?"

"Perhaps," suggested Mr. Willett**'s** *fiancée,* "perhaps he was **a** little bit—jealous."

"I only wish he had reason to be," rejoined Merriman galantly. **"But I** see that you are laughing at me again, Miss Hopkinson. Well, I must get away into **the dark** somewhere **by** myself **and** think out this muddle. Just time to catch my train," he added, looking at his **watch.** "But **if you** are writing to Willett,

you had better advise him to keep out of my
sight for a few days. If he should cross my
war-path while I'm in my present state of
mind, I won't answer for the consequences.
Good-evening, Miss Hopkinson, and—oh, yes,
I had nearly forgotten—*Ich gratuliere.*"

"Good-evening, Mr. Merriman," she said,
extending **her** hand, and, as he took **it,** she
continued, "You must promise me to make
up your quarrel with Hattie. I shall explain
things to her, and you must call on her as
soon as they get back **to** town. Won't you,
now?"

"Yes, I will; and I'm much obliged for
your intercession. She's too good a girl to
have a fight with."

"And, Mr. Merriman, I expect to be in New
York this spring, and should be very glad if
you would call on me, too. Charlie will let
you know where I am, or Mr. Willett."

Merriman's face flushed with pleasure.
"Thank you again. I certainly shall. And,
till then, good-by."

"Good-by," she answered, and added softly,
"till then."

"Till then—till then," he repeated to himself
as the train bore him rapidly through the night
between the river bank and the echoing rocks.
"How do those lines **of** Arnold's go? 'Till
then '—

"Till then her lovely eyes maintain
    Their gay, unwavering, deep disdain."

IV.
DECLARATION OF INDEPENDENCE.

DECLARATION OF INDEPENDENCE.

A Fourth of July Story.

THE haymakers at work in my uncle's side-hill meadows had an original way of telling the noon. They were not the owners of watches, and the church clock was hidden behind the elms, over the tallest of which the top of the white spire, with its lazy vane, could barely be seen. Just at present, too, that sacred time-piece was suffering its semi-annual repairs at the hands of the deliberate Mr. Harriman, the village regulator. No: our chronometer in the hay-field was a simple but admirable combination of horse and hickory-tree. Old Charley, mane-less and all but tailless, long since turned out to grass, used to take refuge from the sun under the shade of this hickory, which stood in the pasture at the foot of the hill. Here he would remain, with his nose to the trunk, switching the flies that settled on his ribs, and, as the shadow wheeled slowly in a shortening radius through the hours of the forenoon, Charley turned with it like a kind of revolving sun-dial, with his nose for a pivot. At noon the shadow thrown by the sparse foliage of the hickory was reduced **to** a round spot on the pasture, leaving large portions of Charley exposed **to** the sun. Then with an impatient whinny, the **old** horse would start for the shelter **of** the red barn across the field, and thereupon the haymakers, hanging their scythes over **the** fence-rail and wiping the sweat **from** their foreheads, would get ready **to take their** nooning.

I was then *ætate* twelve—just the meridian **of** the errand-running age—and so, when Charley made for **the** barn, I would make for the spring where the lunch was kept, treading as far **as** I could **on** the line of the windrows, my bare feet shrinking over the intermediate stubble. **The** spring was under the hill, walled up with stones and shaded by a large chestnut-tree. The meadow thereabout was spongy, and **a** good place to find fringed gentians in October. A basket of bread and cold meat reposed in the shadow, and in the spring itself **bobbed** about some dozen stone bottles filled **with** cider. These bottles, when emptied, became convenient prisons for the little garter-snakes which the haymakers used **to** catch in the long grass. Many are **the** bottled snakes which Cousin Bob and **I** have carried up from the field and let loose among **the** indignant poultry in the hen-yard.

On this particular day I had taken from the cellar some of the best russet cider—*interiore nota*—from behind the big cistern. Each bottle had two raisins in **it** to assist fermentation, and had been laid on its side after being filled, to keep the cork wet. The selection of this choice deposit was a bit of hero-worship on my part : the hay-field was to be honored by a distinguished guest—no less than Cousin Bob himself, who had come all the way from Philadelphia to be present at his sister Kate's wedding.

"It was so kind of you, Bob," said poor Kate, with tears in her eyes, " to come a whole week beforehand and leave all your patients."

" Awful rough on the patients," answered Bob, kissing her in the front hall : "patients under a monument by the time I get back, I guess ; and 'twouldn't make a very large cemetery either."

That was the evening before. Inside the house the family were surrounding Bob in a joyful group. Outside stood the red stage, brilliant in the light that streamed from the parlor windows. The driver was struggling up the walk with Bob's trunk, and I was dancing wildly about under a chaos of valises, dusters, and fishing-rods. A stage-arrival was always an excitement : the arrival of Bob was something to banish sleep for hours. In the watches of the night I longed for the morrow and for Bob's cheery voice shouting, " Shorty, how's 'Old Smoke'? Suppose you get some grease, and we'll go at the barrel." Or else, " Bad hay-weather, Charley ; looks good for pickerel. Suppose you get out the scoop, and we'll try the Pound Brook for live bait right away after grub." And in the morning I awoke to the thought, " Bob's come! He's in the next room. There goes his guitar now."

I jumped out of bed, and dressed like a minute-man of the Revolutionary War or a freshman who hears the last strokes of the prayer-bell. I really believe that Kate's wedding seemed chiefly important to me because it brought old Bob home for a fortnight.

" Come in," said Bob, as I knocked at his door. He was seated superbly on the edge of his bed, clothed upon with his nightshirt as with the toga of old Rome, strumming an accompaniment on his guitar and singing " Rocked in the Cradle of the Deep." His generous bass bore out the song's suggestion of winds and waves and " the wet, blown face of the sea." His deep chest-notes breathed for me the quintessence of all manliness, and even the faces which he had to make when he gave them utterance were of heroic cast—like the tragic masks of the Greek actors. " How you was, old pard? " inquired Bob, unstringing a peg in the guitar. " Do I smell the breakfast in the air, or dooz my eyes deceive my earsight ? "

" I guess it's the waffles," I responded. " We're going to have some." As for Bob's delightful slang, his " daliaunce and fair langáge," I never could answer that except by gleeful and appreciative laughter.

A noise was heard below, as of a bell fiercely wielded but impeded in its vibrations by some wooden obstacle. It was produced by my uncle, who, in his matutinal energy, sought to reinforce the action of the bell by rapping it against the balusters as he rang it. Presently we heard his voice thereunto calling, "Come, get up! Get up! Breakfast! Get up!"

"Ah, *bella—horrida bella!*" said Bob. "There's the governor again. Been at it since cock-crow. Now, I suppose my landlady, with the usual foresight of her sex, has packed my collars and cuffs at the bottom of that trunk. Here, Charley, lend a hand: put those things on the bed." And he handed out in succession half a dozen pairs of boots, a pile of shirts, a box of cigars, a medicine-chest, a powder-flask, a dress-suit, and two or three human bones. "Put those on top—Ossa on Pelion. Begun Latin yet, Charley?"

"Not yet," I answered; "but I'm going to in the fall. Jim Cassidy said I'd better. He says the classicals always lick the Englishers at foot-ball. I'm going into Classical Four. He is in Classical Three now."

"Look out for that box. That's something for Katy." And, after a pause, "Charley, is George Spencer in town?"

"Yes, he is. He came last week. Kennedy says he caught a four-pound bass in the pond Friday; right over by the Point. That's a bully place for bass, Kennedy says. *He* got three there all in an hour," etc., etc.

After breakfast, Bob lighted a cigar and stood with Kate out on the piazza, with his arm round her waist.

" How you do smell of tobacco, Bob!" said **his** sister.

"I suppose, **now, Ketchum** doesn't smoke any?" suggested he.

"Smoking!" exclaimed my uncle, coming to the door and sniffing. "Smoking's **a** foolish and expensive habit. Never smoked in my life. Never used tobacco in any form." And he vanished within. We could hear him as he **went** through the house and left all the doors open behind him, and we laughed.

"Charley," said Bob, "never smoke. **Be** virtuous, and you'll be happy.

' I'll never smoke tobacco, **no.** It is a filthy
    weed.
  I'll never smoke tobacco, no,' says little Robert
    Reed.

Bless you, my child, bless you!"

"Now, Bob, how can you make fun of pa in that disrespectful way? And, besides, you are just encouraging Charley to learn the habit when he gets older ; and you know father wants him **not** to."

Katy had **been** a little nervous and petulant of late. Bob made no reply, but puffed reflectively.

"Jim Cassidy smokes catalpas," I volunteered ; "and he isn't but six months older than me ; and he said his father saw him smoking one the other day, and he just laughed."

"Frightful levity in **a** parent!" said Bob.

"Aren't you looking a little thin, Katy?" he went on, squeezing her waist a bit.

"I don't know but I am," answered Katy listlessly. My cousin was a tall girl and very pretty. She had rosy cheeks and gray eyes, and a large, sweet mouth.

"By the way," continued Bob, a little awkwardly, "Charley says that George Spencer has come home."

Kate said nothing in response.

"Charley!" I heard my aunt's voice calling to me from the back yard.

"Yes, in a minute," I shouted. "Cousin Bob, I've got to go down to the hay-field now and take the lunch. You're coming down by and by, aren't you?"

"Any cider left?"

"Yes, some bully—russet cider."

"Well," said Bob, "I'll come down about noon."

"All right. They're mowing the heater lot to-day." And I started around the house.

Accordingly, when the old horse struck twelve in the manner which I have described, and just as I was lifting the cider-bottles from the spring and the haymakers were gathering under the apple-tree in the lower part of the field, I saw Bob vault the bars and come down the hill. At the same time a buggy stopped at another set of bars. It was drawn by Dick, successor to Charley, and bore my uncle and Mr. Ketchum, the gentleman who was to marry my cousin Kate. After "hanging" the horse to the post,

they also came down through the meadow, and
we all met at the spring.   Bob and Mr.
Ketchum shook hands.

"How **are** you, Ketchum ?   **My** congratulations."

"Thank you, doctor, thank **you.**   Kate said
you were coming on the stage last night, and
you must excuse me for not having been at the
house to meet you.   **I** had some important
business at the Farms.   I'm trying to get my
business all done up this week.   Business before
pleasure, you know."

"Yes, of course ; don't mention **it.**   Did you
drive down with the governor ?"

"With—— I beg your pardon."

"With my father.   Of course you did, though.
I saw you get out."   Bob laughed constrainedly,
and turned to shake hands with his old friends
among the men, who had seated themselves at
a respectful distance and were waiting for their
lunch.

My uncle was a smooth-shaved, stoutish man,
with **a** face of a uniform red color.   He carried
a rough apple-tree stick.   He stood with great
emphasis on the ground (*his* ground), with jaw
dropped and eyes asquint in the sun, regarding
the mowing-machine, which came clicking up
through its last swath and stopped at some distance off.   "Grass in that holler pretty thin,
ain't it ?" he shouted to the driver.

"Wal, *'tis* kind **o'** light.   There's a piece in
the middle you'll have to cut with the scythes,
I guess."

"Cut it with scythes? What's that for? Don't want any peckin' round with scythes. Men got enough to do along the fences."

"Wal, I can't go in there with the machine. It's too rough. Scratch it all to thunder—Whoa, there!"

"Rough! What makes it rough?"

"Stuns makes it rough."

"Stones! Stones in there? That's some of McFadden's shiftless work. I told him to get 'em all out last fall and pile 'em on the wall. Gave him gunpowder to blast 'em with."

"Wal, squire, guess he used your gunpowder up shootin' woodchucks, then. He left an almighty pile of stuns in that holler, anyway."

This conversation was carried on in a shout. Then the mowing-machine started up its click and went off across the meadow. My uncle's little blue eyes continued to squint in a mechanical way over the landscape. Suddenly they settled on me in the immediate foreground: "Halloo! shoo-shoo! Where's your boots? Mustn't go barefoot. Dirty trick! Mustn't go barefoot. Get your feet cut: get the lock-jaw."

I retired slowly toward the red barn, where my shoes and stockings were stowed away on a beam, and as I went I ruminated. My uncle seldom interfered in my education. He left that to the women, *i. e.*, to Aunt Sophia and Cousin Kate. His attentions to me were usually confined to sudden warnings about the

danger of walking on the picket-fence or climbing the barn roof. " Hi ! **hi !**" he would shout
from some coign of vantage—the wood-shed
door, for instance—" mustn't fool round the
horse. Get kicked." He often gave me six-
pences and asked me if I should like to be a
lawyer when I grew up. Only on one occasion
had he taken **my** education directly in hand,
and that was when it had suddenly occurred to
him that my æsthetic culture was being
neglected. " Don't play on any musical instrument, do you ? " he inquired. " I used to play
the fife myself **when** I was a boy. Don't read
any poetry, do you ? Come into the office, and
I'll give you a copy of ' Hudibras.' Got four
or five."

A single anecdote will illustrate sufficiently
my uncle's fitness **to** guide unæsthetic youth
into the higher realms of imagination, and will
show how much sympathy he was likely to have
with the sentimental grievances of those under
his control. Cousin Bob—who fancied himself
something **of a** connoisseur in painting—had
picked **up, at a** dealer's **in** Philadelphia, some
half-dozen little oils which he affirmed rather
vaguely **to** be " originals." They represented
various saints and martyrs of all degrees of
maceration. They were visible only in a strong
light, the background and the raiment of the
holy men having seemingly been reduced by
smoke to a uniform blackness, against which
stood out here and there **a** leaden face or a
sallow and emaciated leg. These cheerful

effigies **Bob** **brought** **out** **of** **his** **trunk** **when**
home **on a** visit, and, after having explained
their points to Aunt Sophia, who put **full** faith
in them, and to Kate, who laughed **at** them, **he**
hung them—without frames—on the walls **of**
his room, where **they** remained after his departure. Bob's **room was** over **my** uncle's
office. It was **a** sacred apartment, always
reserved for him and retaining a faint odor of
tobacco-smoke. **The** mantelpiece was littered
with glorious *vestigia* **of** its occupant, such **as**
old pipes, sword-belts, rusty fishing-reels, and
surgical instruments, which were never disturbed. **I** sometimes penetrated to the seclu-
sion of this chamber, inhaled its subtle aroma,
so suggestive **of** dear old absent **Bob**, and
gazed upon the ghostly presences which **be-**
decked the walls. These, as originals, inspired
me with a mysterious respect, and not **for** the
kingdoms of this earth would I have dreamed
of laying sacrilegious hands on them. But one
day—oh, my prophetic soul ! my uncle !—my
uncle, I say, had brought a house-painter on
the premises. After **he** had painted the well-
curb, the fence in the front yard, the red
benches in the back **stoop, the** green shutters
of the milk-room, etc., **my** uncle, ransacking
the house with his accustomed energy in search
of further objects needing repair, lighted on
Bob's saints. **" Here,"** he shouted **to the**
painter from the top **of** the office staircase,
" here ! come up here ! Suppose you touch up
these picters. Give 'em a coat or two apiece ;

make 'em look pretty : faded out so you can't
see what they look like."

I had followed uncle,—having made friends
with the painter, who conversed affably with
me while he plied his brush all **the** forenoon,—
and **I** now stood rigid with horror, regarding
alternately the red face of this avuncular Vandal
and the parchment visages of his intended vic-
tims. " But, uncle," **I** faltered, " Bob used to
say that the dark colors were all the beauty of
these paintings."

" Don't want any beauty of 'em here. Dingy
old things ! Touch **'em** up **a** bit. Brighten
'em up, so folks can see what they are. When
you get through, come down into the office and
I'll pay you."

Then did that smearer of barns, without a
misgiving,—nay, even with a simple faith in the
resources of his art which begat in me a kind
of confidence,—proceed to adorn Bob's originals
with fresh garments. To the mantle of one he
imparted a brave vermilion, using the very
pigment with which he had daubed the benches
in the **stoop.** The girdle which bound the
withered loins of a dying eremite was painted a
living green—the green of the milk-room
shutters. Only a doubt as to the precise nature
of the aureole which encircled the head of one
glorified martyr saved that mystic circle from a
coat of the best brown paint. And, finally,
each leathery cheek received, exactly at its
centre, a hectic bloom of the shape and diameter
of the old-fashioned copper cent. And then

the artist, having surveyed his work with honest pride, picked up his paint-pots and descended into the office to receive his ill-gotten gains. I rushed at once to my cousin Kate and dragged her to the scene. She laughed till her pretty eyes were full of tears, and sank gasping into a chair. The comments of Bob on his next visit home were brief flut emphatic. The restored originals disappeared forever.

Well, I had put on my shoes and stockings and returned to the spring just as Bob was opening the first bottle of cider, when a man was seen coming up the hill with a gun over his shoulder and a game-bag slung under his arm.

"Halloa!" cried Bob, looking up, "there comes George Spencer. What has he been after? Woodcock? To-day is the 1st of July, that's a fact, and the law is off." Spencer bowed as he passed us, a few rods away, and was going on up the hill, when Bob sung out, "O George! You aren't going to give me the go-by, are you?"

"Why, doctor, how are you?" responded Spencer, stopping suddenly and approaching us. "I'm glad to see you home; indeed I am."

He shook hands warmly with Bob, and bowed stiffly to Mr. Ketchum and my uncle, the latter of whom simply glared at him in return and then faced about and fixed his eye on some distant point in the valley. The new-comer was a tall, boyish looking young man, with a careless, not to say slouching, gait, but graceful withal, and having a merry blue eye with just a bit of the devil in it, and an expression of face as of one who took the world perhaps too easily.]

"Any sport?" asked Bob, pointing to the game-pouch.

"These," answered Spencer, taking out some half-dozen small bodies, mostly feathers and bill; "the spoils of the chase," he added with a laugh.

"Oh, golly!" I began, fired with the predatory instinct and regardless of possible snubs, "you ought to see the bag Dave Brown had, day before yesterday, coming out of Parson's cover. Sixteen woodcock and——"

"Look out, Charley," broke in my cousin: "don't be giving Dave away. Mr. Ketchum is in the legislature, you know, and has to look out for the game-laws."

"Day before yesterday was Sunday," said the law-maker in question, with an accent of disapproval.

"That's it," said I. "Dave Brown says Sundays don't count in law. He says——"

"Charley!" shouted my uncle, "here! Take this basket down to the men, and ask 'em if they have got enough cider."

Spencer glanced up with a look half of annoyance and half of amusement. His face flushed slightly, and he dropped the birds back into the pouch, and saying, "Well, I must be off," turned and pursued his way over the field just as I was moving reluctantly off on my errand.

It was not **so** much **what my uncle had said,** but the tone in which **he said it implied** that he didn't want me in Spencer's company. I hurried back to the spring in time to hear him say, **"I** thought that fellow was gone to New York for good—gone to be an architect, **or** something."

"I suppose he **is** taking **a little** vacation," ventured Bob.

"Taking a vacation, hey **?"** said **my** uncle, with **a** snort. "Better stick to his **work.** Young men take **too** many vacations now-adays."

"I'm **afraid,"** said **Mr.** Ketchum, with slow and mournful unction, "that it's vacation **with** Spencer pretty much **all** the time. I'm afraid he won't make architecture go. **He is** too unstable : 'unstable as water, he will not excel,' **as** the good book says. Now, **I** spoke to him, **before** he went to New York, about making **the** plans for **an** extension we are building to the mill ; **I** wanted to give **him a** lift ; but he didn't seem to take any interest, and my partners got sick **of** waiting for him, and gave the **job** to another man. What a man wants, to succeed in business, is concentration. Spencer scatters himself—goes **round** playing chess, and botanizing, and tooting **on a** French horn, and all that sort of fooling. He doesn't bring himself **to a** focus, like he ought."

"He's a poor toad," pronounced my uncle sententiously, and **with an air** as though Mr.

Ketchum was refining too curiously on **a sub-**ject unworthy of such metaphysical analysis.

Bob seemed uncomfortable under this criticism of Spencer, and it was no less than shocking **to** me, **in** whose system of hero-worship that over-versatile genius occupied a place second only to Bob himself. Was not his prowess with rod and gun acknowledged even by **Dave** Brown—him, **the** unsabbatical, the scorner **of** statute law, the profane and bibulous **brother of** the angle—who frequently in my **own** hearing **had** borne testimony to George's gift, **as** he sat and spat among a crowd of idlers on the stoop of the Eagle Hotel.

"**Thar's the** Hinmans," Dave would say: "they gits *some* trouts, but I kin beat them. Thar's Joe Briggs: he's a pretty good fisherman; he gits *some* trouts, but I can beat *him*. Thar's Willem Holt—comes up from 'York—he thinks **he** knows how to fish. Wal, he gits *some* trouts. **But** I kin beat the hull on 'em by ——! Me *and* George Spencer kin beat the hull d——n lot of 'em !"

It was this Crichton of a Spencer who had taught me how to cast **a** fly and to construct a sucker-trap. He had a canoe on the river, and had given me lessons in paddling. Once he even lent me **his** double-barreled shot-gun—under conditions of **the** strictest secrecy and caution in handling, on my **part.** He could whittle anything out of wood, and he had made an elegant model in soap-stone of St. Swithin's Church, which was quite the gem of the church-fair where it was raffled for. He would dash you off pen-and-ink caricatures of all the queer people in the village. And how often at night, when passing his mother's little white house, had I listened with rapture to the strains of George's French horn, where his lonely taper glimmered late among the pines! And then, too, what an admirable woman was Mrs. Spencer, the mother, and how toothsome the vergalieu pears in her side-yard!

But I knew, though rather vaguely, why my uncle was down on this hero of mine. I am telling this story *ab extra*, and solely from recollection of what I myself saw and heard. I will not vouch for hearsay evidence, and I was not of an age when one is usually taken into family councils; nor should I have taken much interest in the sentimental woes of my elders, having in especial a boy's contempt for young women and their love-affairs. But thus much I partly knew and partly guessed: George Spencer and my cousin Kate had been sweethearts, and their passion had been frowned on by my uncle, who, in an angry interview with the young man, had spoken most disrespectfully of his "prospects," and had ended by forbidding Kate to see him. This in itself might not have been enough to break off the affair, for Kate was a spirited girl, with a large share of inherited obstinacy; but there had followed some misunderstanding between the lovers. Whether Kate thought that George took his dismissal by her father too

proudly and kept away from her in consequence, or whether he thought that she took it
too lightly and consoled herself too readily by
flirtations with her other admirers, I never
quite knew. Kate certainly was a little of a
coquette, as indeed she had a right to be, being
the **acknowledged** belle of the village and
much sought after by the young men at picnics
and hops. Poor George took it hard enough.
I used to meet him **in the** dusk, mooning fur-
tively about the outskirts of our orchard, and
to wonder what he was at. It has since occurred to me that he was watching the light in
Kate's window—as time out of mind has been
lovers' wont—and that the apple-tree shadows
were to him in lieu of those " broom groves
whose shade the dismissed bachelor loves."

And once he bribed me with the sum of
fifty cents, to me in hand paid, to give him an
old photograph of Kate and say nothing about
it to anyone—a bargain which seemed to me
advantageous beyond the wildest dreams of
" swaps " and speculations in jack-knives or
rabbit-coops. Kate, too, moped badly at first.
She chose melancholy airs for her piano. She
had redness of the eyes—like the drunkards of
Ephraim ; and I used to find scraps of Byronic
verse on her writing-table and evidently of her
own composition, beginning :

Oh, there are times in life's dull dream.

Alas! this was in ante-Tennyson days, when
L. E. L. was still in vogue ; and Kate was not

without a strong dash of romance in an otherwise very healthy and sensible temperament.

After a while she came out of this mood and was quite gay again ; and finally, after a desperate flirtation with Mr. Ketchum, she engaged herself to that gentleman with her father's full approval—my aunt Sophia, as usual, acquiescent rather than enthusiastic. Mr. Ketchum was quite the rising young man of our village. He had a third share in the large cotton-mill at Whistleville. He was of an inventive turn, and owned the patent of several agricultural implements, which brought him in a very pretty plum. He was our postmaster, and had represented the town twice in the State legislature. It was mainly through his public-spirited exertions that the railroad extension to the neighboring town of Whistleville had been procured. He was Sunday-school superintendent and junior warden of St. Swithin's Church, of which my uncle was senior warden. He was reckoned rather a handsome man, too, with his luxuriant side-whiskers, black eyes, and big red lips. His manners were even excessive. If my aunt Sophia or any lady entered the room where he was sitting in an arm-chair, he would rise and insist upon her taking his seat. Once, when he dined at our house, I was greatly impressed by the delicacy which he showed in holding his handkerchief before his face, as a screen, while he picked his teeth. And yet, in spite of these unquestioned virtues, I knew that

Bob was never quite reconciled to **Mr.** Ketchum's engagement with Kate. But **if** asked to name his objection, he always put it on some absurd ground as, for instance, that Ketchum wore cloth shoes—which was quite as unreasonable as Petruchio's motive for throwing his wine-sops in the sexton's face. As **for** cloth shoes, **Mr.** Ketchum certainly dressed elegantly, wearing a black frock and a **tall** hat, even on week-days. His affable prosperity had never seemed in stronger contrast with poor George's prospectless condition than **now,** while the latter, in his faded brown coat and seedy trousers, was climbing slowly up the hill toward the bars that led out of the meadow into the Whistleville turnpike. His very back, as he walked, had **a** dispirited and almost loaferish expression.

But now the only absent **member of** my *dramatis personæ* came on the scene—the heroine herself, who, with a wide straw hat on her head and **a** bunch of pansies in her belt, appeared on the other side of the bars just as Spencer reached them from the field. We could see the quondam lover raise his hat and let down the bars for **her** to pass. We could see Kate smile ; we could see that they exchanged a word or two, as she stepped through the gate and came toward us down the smooth green slope, while he replaced **the** bars and went up the road. Only a word or two, but it proved to be enough. Balzac tells of a quickwitted demoiselle who could *dépêcher une acco-*

lade while mounting the staircase behind her duenna.

Kate was humming a tune as she approached the group by the spring. She had a heightened color and a conscious look about the mouth. Her eyes, cast down demurely, seemed looking for some wild flower along the shaven meadow-ground.

"Well, good-morning, Miss Kate," began Ketchum, taking her by the arm with an air of ownership which she seemed a little to resent. "Come tagging after the men, have you? Couldn't keep away from us. No; I thought not. That's the way with the ladies all. Isn't that so, doctor?"

Mr. Ketchum, though a man of business habits and a Sunday-school superintendent, was by no means a person of severe and gloomy mien. He often said that, in his view, religion should be a cheerful and not an ascetic thing. In his business he found it more profitable to be "genial" than "stuck up." Though not "a drinking man," as he would explain, he would take a drink upon occasion with commercial or political acquaintances, and would himself insist upon "setting 'em up all round" with hospitable iteration whenever the business in hand required such lubricants. Though holding strict views touching the observance of the Sabbath, he was, on the whole, a progressive and liberal spirit, and in the famous contention in St. Swithin's Church as to the propriety of singing operatic selections, he held

with the popular side.   He was secretly adored
by the young ladies **of** the choir and of **the**
Sunday school, who esteemed his air of mingled gallantry and playfulness the perfection of
high-bred **wit, to** be met on their part only
with applausive giggles and cries of, "Oh, Mr.
Ketchum, *do* stop making me laugh! You're
too funny!" **etc.,** etc.

But to-day this excellent fooling was for
some reason thrown away on Bob, who sullenly declined response to Ketchum's appeal,
and made as though he heard it not, ransacking
the hamper in silence **to** find the corkscrew.

"We saw you talking with Spencer at the
fence," pursued the humorist, winking at the
unresponsive Bob. "I guess I shall have to
be looking after Spencer. Come, now, tell us
what he said. Did he promise to dance at the
wedding?"

"Oh, fiddlesticks!" said Kate, disengaging
her arm and darting a look expressive of rather
complicated emotions at her prospective bride-
groom. "I want some lunch. Is there any
pie, pa?"

"No pie here. Don't want any such flummery round here. Good, plain bread and
meat, cider, boiled eggs," answered my uncle,
with his mouth full of the last-named item.

"Come, step up to the counter and ask the
squire for a glass of cider," urged Ketchum.

"Cider goes to my head," answered Kate,
with a pout; "but I want a sandwich—and,
Charley, get me a glass of spring water, please.

Bob, you bad **boy,** what made **you run off** just after breakfast ? I've scarcely seen **you** yet, and I've **got lots of** things **to** talk **to you** about."

" Fire away," **said Bob,** who had found the corkscrew and was opening a fresh bottle.

" **Well,**" remarked **Mr.** Ketchum, consulting his watch, " time's up with me, **so I'll** clear out and **give** you a chance. **I know Kate** has got lots **of** things to talk to me about, **too, but** she's too bashful **to** say them before company. **So you'll** have **to be** patient, Katy, and keep 'em till next week."

" Oh, go along with you," replied **she.** " I haven't *anything* to say to you—not anything at all."

One perceives that our poor Kate was nothing of a Beatrice, and had little else at command in the shape of repartee than **the** sauciness of any old-fashioned Yankee girl.

" Well, good-morning, **Mr.** Craig; good-morning **all.** Ta-ta, Katy; keep up your spirits, **and try** to get along without me for a while." And **Mr.** Ketchum took himself off.

Presently, Kate put her arm into Bob's and strolled down into the pastures, leaning against his shoulder, talking and laughing. My uncle had already started for a distant corner of the hay-field, **to** examine a fence that needed repairs, and thus the lunch party broke up.

The wedding was appointed for the tenth of July. On the evening of the Fourth there were fireworks **on** the village green. Our house

fronted on this center **of** disturbance and, as
soon as it grew dark, the family and many
neighbors assembled on the piazza and in the
yard, which was filled with chairs and settees,
prepared to witness what the local press afterward described as a " grand pyrotechnic dis-
play." The scene, in sooth, was not without
its qualities. In the middle of the green was
a platform thickly sown with torches, by whose
smoky glare an infuriated brass band per-
formed discords. The Eagle Hotel was brilliant with candles in every window, and its
stoop was crowded with the sturdy yeomanry
of the vicinage. Fantastic lights and shadows
flickered over the turf, and a ring of darkness
shut in the whole, save where a few Chinese
lanterns twinkled among the trees of some
patriot's door-yard. Into this outer blackness
the fireworks cast momentary illuminations ;
and here, upon the skirts of the village, the
boys lay in wait for the dropping of the rocket-
sticks, useful in the construction of kites. I
was in those days a keen hunter of the rocket-
stick, and, though larger game may since have
crossed my path, I am ready to maintain that
there is an excitement in that mystic nocturnal
chase which nothing in later life can quite
supply. The flight of a rocket ! You wait in
the shadow with a beating heart, till suddenly
—a rush—a scream, and the noble creature
sails heavenward with the deliberate grace of a
serpent or an eagle, hovers an instant above the
world in a column of dissolving fire, and then

a soft explosion, and a few lambent stars, crimson and green and violet, come dropping earthward through the summer night; and away we go after them, plunging into the dark, with eyes fixed on the course of the meteors and ears straining for the thud of the sticks as they hit the ground. Sometimes they fall on a roof, sometimes in a pond—and then I have known the entire hunt to leap in after them, clothes and all, in the heat of the chase.

On this particular evening I had been unlucky, and had secured only one short stick. I was posted alone in a field north of the green, near the Whistleville pike, and most of the rockets had taken a different direction. For half an hour there had been nothing put off but blue-lights, pin-wheels, and such small deer. I had begun to despair of further prey, and had just made up my mind to strike out for home and claim my share of the lemonade and sponge-cake which I knew that Hannah was to distribute among the spectators in our front yard, when—*f-r-s-h!*—the blackness overhead was cleft as by an arrow of flame. The head burst just above me, and the sticks descended toward the north side of the field.

"By the mighty, I've got 'em!" I chortled in my joy, and started across the field on a run. Farther yet—farther! They'll drop beyond the fence, perhaps in the road, perhaps in the next lot. And, indeed, just as I reached the fence the sticks fell. They struck the top of a carriage

that was driving along the road, and frightened
the horses so that they reared and plunged.
The night was dark, but I could see the figure
of a man standing at the horses' heads, and I
heard from the carriage a woman's voice—a
voice that I knew—saying, in a low, agitated
tone, " Oh, George, what was it ? Take me
back ! please take me back ! I wish I hadn't
come."

And then I heard the man—whose voice I
recognized also—answer soothingly, " It's nothing, darling : nothing but one of those cursed
rocket-sticks, that startled the horses a bit.
But they are all quiet now. They're perfectly
gentle. Don't be afraid, dear. Keep hold of
the reins a minute till I jump in."

And in a trice he was in the carriage, and
the team was off down the road at full speed.
It had all happened so quickly that I had had
no time to think what it meant. I had even
forgotten the rocket-sticks, till the tramp of feet
and a rush of boys across the field recalled my
mind to the quarry, which had now somehow
lost its importance.

" Say, young feller," the foremost called out,
" did them sticks fall anywheres round
here ? "

" In the road, somewhere," I answered indifferently. And, leaving them to search for them,
I hurried home and joined the circle in the front
yard.

" Where is Kate ? " I whispered, as soon as
I had picked out my aunt Sophia from among

the mothers in Israel who were purring gently in the back seats.

"Kate went into the house with a headache, Charley, some time ago. Perhaps you had better go and see how she is, and ask her if I can do anything for her."

I ran upstairs and knocked at Kate's door. No one answered. I opened the door. The room was empty, and the lamp burning. Then I looked for Bob, and found him at the front gate, making himself agreeable to a local young woman.

"Cousin Bob," I said, "come into the house, please, a moment. Something important."

"Important! Been blowing your fingers off with a toy cannon?"

"No. Please come in. Really and truly it's important. Come."

Bob excused himself and followed me into the hall.

"Kate has run off," I said breathlessly.

"What do you mean?"

"With George Spencer," I added.

"Where? When? Who told you so?"

I explained as rapidly as I could.

"Come into the office," said Bob.

We found my uncle seated at his desk, writing. The front door was sternly closed, that he might seem to lend no countenance to the fireworks, which he disapproved of as frivolous and dangerous inventions, liable to set fire to barns and other property—whereby plaintiff hath suffered great damage.

" Tell him what you saw, Charley," said Bob.

I entered upon my narrative, my uncle listening with a dazed expression, and when I had finished, breaking out with, " Hey ! What? Kate in **a** wagon? Who with? Spencer? Where was she going ? "

" Toward Whistleville."

" Whistleville? What **for ?** "

I hesitated, and Bob came to my relief : " Why, **it is** very **clear, sir, I** think, that the girl has run off."

" Run off ! Flummery ! What would she want to run off for ! The boy has made a mistake. Kate is out looking at the fireworks. Saw her myself half an hour ago."

" No," I cried eagerly, " Aunt Sophia says she went into the house some time ago with a headache ; and I looked in her room, and she wasn't there."

" Then she is just taking a little drive. Run **off !** What should make her run off ? Stuff and nonsense ! " But he rose from his desk with an anxious look and grasped the appletree stick that stood **in the** corner by his chair.

" I'm afraid it's more than that, sir," said Bob gravely. " Kate has been acting queer the last few days. She's too good a girl to do anything in a premeditated way that would give us all pain. But, then, the best girls have romantic notions, and she may have given way all of a sudden. She used to be very fond of Spencer at one time, you know ; and it isn't likely—is it ?—that they would be just taking a drive all for nothing at this hour of the evening."

"The miserable hound!" shouted my uncle, suddenly experiencing conviction and displaying an equally sudden energy. "Tell William to put Dick into the buggy—quick! Charley, run over to the post-office and tell Ketchum to come right over here. Send your aunt into the office."

"Hold up a bit," said Bob. "Dick's no good. We want the fastest pair they've got at the livery stable, and a light wagon. Charley, dust out and order Scott to put in the best team he has got. I'll follow you there in a minute. And if I were you, sir, I wouldn't notify Ketchum or say anything at all to mother. There's no use making a scandal, and it may be I can overtake them before the 10.35 train leaves Whistleville. They must be meaning to catch that. Time enough to kick up a bobbery if they get off."

"Do what you like, Bob," answered his father, sinking into his chair with an air of utter collapse.

"Run ahead, Charley," said Bob. "I'll take you with me. You had better stay in the office, sir, till we get back, and act as if nothing had happened. I'll go up and lock Kate's door and tell mother that she is asleep, and not to disturb her."

At this point I left the office, and cannot say what further conversation passed between father and son. But when Bob joined me at

Scott's stables, some fifteen minutes later, he reported, with a shake of the head, that the governor was badly cut up.

Our team was a fast one, and hardly needed the cut of the whip that my cousin gave them as we turned into the Whistleville road. The night was dark and warm. The trees and bushes went by with a rush, and I had such a wild feeling of adventure that I could scarcely keep from shouting aloud as Bob put the ribbons into my hands, while he lighted a cigar, and said, "Let 'em spin, Shorty! Give 'em head. They've got at least half an hour's start," he added, as he resumed the reins. Beyond this we exchanged no words about our errand, but bowled along in silence, having that shamefaced reticence in matters sentimental which prevails between a man and a boy. It was five miles to Whistleville. We had gone about half the distance, and had reached the top of a bare hill, when Bob pulled up abruptly. "Hark!" he exclaimed. "Is that the sound of wheels ahead?"

We both listened intently.

"No," I answered; "it's only the brook down in the hollow."

"Pshaw! So it is," said Bob—"Get up!"

But, at the instant of starting, one of the hind-wheels rolled gently from its axle, the carriage toppled over on its side in a leisurely manner, and I found myself lying among the sweet-fern and huckleberry-bushes by the road-side. The horses stood perfectly still. There was a moment of silence, and then—"Damn everything!" said Bob, from the ditch. He had kept hold of the reins, and neither of us was hurt, as the carriage, luckily, had no headway on and the fall was soft. "Strike a match, Charley, and look at my watch. I can't let go the reins."

"It is a quarter past ten," I reported, after some fumbling.

"The game is up," said Bob.

"It's only two miles and a quarter," I suggested; "couldn't we hoof it?"

"What! in twenty minutes? Not much we couldn't. We had just about time enough to make it with the wagon."

"We might get another wagon from a farmer."

"There's nothing but woods for a mile ahead. No; about face! The next time you see your cousin Kate, young man, her name will be Mrs. Spencer."

We unhitched the sweating team, drew the carriage off the road, and started homeward on foot, Bob leading the horses and whistling softly as he went. About half a mile up the road we came to a farmhouse, where the lights were still burning. Here we got a pole, and, putting in the horses, drove back to the village. It was near midnight when we reached the green, and the Fourth was over. A smell of gunpowder still lingered in the air, but the houses were dark, except where a few sleepless revelers kept wassail in the barroom of the

Eagle Hotel. **We left** the horses at the **stable,**
and went directly **to** my uncle's office, where
a light **was** burning. Bob shrank perceptibly
from entering.   There were voices inside, and,
as we opened the door and walked in, we found
Mr. Ketchum in the act of taking leave. He
evidently knew nothing of what had happened,
for his face wore its habitual look of smug self-
satisfaction.   My uncle, on the contrary, had an
expression of ill-concealed nervousness, which
deepened into alarm as his eye sought Bob's
for tidings of our success.   Bob shook his head.
No one spoke.

Mr. Ketchum saw **that** something was the
matter. "Anything   wrong?" he inquired,
looking from **one** to the other.   "Anybody
sick?"

"Sit down **a** minute, Ketchum ; sit down,"
said my poor uncle.   He made one or two efforts
to speak, but his voice shook so that he could
hardly utter a word. Finally, he controlled
himself, and began, " I hoped it would turn out
a mistake, or that we could stop it in time, and
so I said nothing to you. But—but—I am
terribly shocked—terribly mortified to have to
tell you.   My daughter has acted badly ; she
has disgraced her father. You can't feel worse
about it than I do."

" For Heaven's sake, what's the matter ? " demanded Ketchum.

" Oh, let's have it out," broke in Bob, stepping
forward.   " Ketchum, she has run away with
George Spencer,—this evening, while the fire-

works were going on. They went to Whistleville, and I went after them as soon as we discovered it; but the wagon broke down on top
of Moss' Hill,—and so they've got off; and,
upon my soul, I'm sorry for it, and I didn't
think it of Kate. If she wanted to break with
you, she might have done it fair and square.
This running off in the dark is a shabby business. The girl has treated you badly, Ketchum,
and the family owes you an apology."

Bob held out his hand, but Mr. Ketchum did
not appear to notice it. His face went white and
red by starts, and the passions of grief, anger,
and shame chased each other over his broad
cheeks like flying cloud-shadows across a
meadow. "Why didn't you tell me this when
I came in here to-night?" he demanded at
length, facing my uncle.

"I thought Bob might catch the fools and
bring 'em back in time to save this disgrace
and hush the thing up," explained the run-
away's parent.

"Oh! And you thought the girl was good
enough for me anyway, even if she had run off
with another feller."

"There was time to catch 'em; there was
time to stop it, before they could get the down
train, if the wagon hadn't broke down. Mean,
stinking wagons Scott always keeps!" he
added, with a parenthetic rage.

"Oh, the wagon broke down, did it?"
sneered Ketchum, with a black look at Bob.
"Yes; I've heard of that kind of wagon before.

I'll tell you what it is, Squire Craig; I can see when a job is put **up** on me as well as the next man, and I ain't going **to** swallow **it** so sweet **and** nice."

" What **do** you mean by that, **sir ? "** said my uncle.

" I mean that I may not be a college-educated **man or** belong **to a** high-toned family, but as long as you felt sure I had the stamps, you was glad enough to take me all the same, and so **was** the girl. But as soon as this report about **the mill** gets around, you shake me quick as a wink. And the joke is on you, after all. For, **as sure** as I **sit** here, that story about **our** paper's being protested in Thimblebury is a darned rotten lie, and the man that started it knows it's a darned lie." And he brought his fist down on the table with an emphasis on the expletive that lent it almost the dignity of an oath, and doubtless gave its utterer a delightful thrill of wickedness.

" So help me God !" said my uncle, after a pause, " I never heard any report of that kind till this minute, and it wouldn't have made a particle of difference with me if I had. I didn't want your money, and my daughter didn't want your money. **I** favored the match myself because I thought you a worthy, industrious young man of good principles and steady habits."

" It's a put-up job," asserted Ketchum, rising and taking his hat from the table. " I don't say that you are in it yourself, Mr. Craig—and **I** dare say you aint ; but your daughter is, clear enough, and so is her brother. Well, I wish you joy of your son-in-law—a cuss without a cent, and that don't know how to make a cent for the life of him. As for that little flirt——"

"There," broke in Bob; "that'll do. Not another word. I took you for a gentleman, and I made you an apology accordingly, which I see I didn't owe you ; but if you say anything——"

"Bob !" interrupted my uncle authoritatively. And, as Ketchum stalked out of the office, he continued, "The man has been insulting, but he has a right to feel hard toward us. Kate has treated him shamefully ; she has treated the whole of us shamefully."

"Well," replied Bob, breathing short, "I don't defend the way she did it, but I'm glad she's done it, after all. That fellow is a cad to the bottom of him. I always thought so, and now I know it. Spencer's a gentleman, if he isn't anything else."

"Halloo !" exclaimed my uncle, recovering his usual manner as his eye fell on me. "What's the boy doing here? No place for boys. Time to be abed. Here,—here's a dollar for your savings bank; buy fire-crackers next Fourth. Off to bed with you." And I withdrew.

Here is the letter which my tearful Aunt Sophia received from Kate a day or two later. I found it last week in a bundle of yellow papers in the little hair-cloth trunk under the garret stairs. *Eheu fugaces!*

NEW YORK, July, 6, 18—.

MY DEAR, DEAR MOTHER : Will you ever forgive me ? You must, for I am so happy. I know that I have done very, very wrong, but George **was so** impetuous. He had a presentiment that, unless I went with him that night, we never should be married. You know what a strong *will* father has, and I did not dare to face the *scene* that would have taken place if I had broken off my engagement with Mr. Ketchum in the usual way. Poor Mr. Ketchum ! I have treated him very badly, and I *did* like him—in **a** way. But, mother, I found that I could *not* marry him. He was too vulgar. Only think **!** I discovered that he had bought a book called ' Etiquette and Eloquence ; **or,** The Perfect Gentleman,' telling about how to behave in company, etc.; and he used to learn little speeches out of it and say them **to me** when he called. Please all of you forgive me, and write to me at No. 137 Blank Street, where we are boarding. George has a good situation with his uncle, who is an architect and is going to take him into partnership some day. I wish you could see how happy I am.

Ever your own loving daughter,

CATHERINE C. SPENCER.

P. S.—We were married that evening at Whistleville, by Rev. Dr. Quickly, in ten minutes. We have heard of poor Bob's accident with the wagon. Dear Bob ! how **I** love him ! Ask him to pardon us for it.

It is needless to add that everyone came round **in** time,—even my uncle, who held out manfully for several months. Even Mr.

Ketchum, if he did not forgive, at least forgot so far as to marry a rich young woman of Thimblebury, with whom he subsequently moved to that flourishing burg and to higher spheres of usefulness in business life.

V.

SPLIT ZEPHYR.

V.

SPLIT ZEPHYR.

An attenuated yarn spun by the Fates.

T was the evening of Commencement Day. The old Church on the green, which had rung for many consecutive hours with the eloquence of slim young gentlemen in evening dress, exhorting the Scholar in Politics or denouncing the Gross Materialism of the Age, was at last empty and still. As it drew the dewy shadows softly about its eaves and filled its rasped interior with soothing darkness, it bore a whimsical likeness to some aged horse which, having been pestered all day with flies, was now feeding in peace along the dim pasture.

It was Clay who suggested this resemblance, and we all laughed appreciatively, as we used to do in those days at Clay's clever sayings. There were five of us strolling down the diagonal walk to our farewell supper at " Ambrose's." Arrived at that refectory, we found it bare of guests and had things quite to ourselves. After supper, we took our coffee out in the little courtyard, where a fountain dribbled, and the flutter of the grape leaves on the trellises in the night wind invited to confidences.

"Well, Armstrong," began Doddridge, "where are you going **to** spend the vacation?"

"Vacation!" answered Armstrong; "vacations are over for me."

"You're **not** going to work for your living at once?" inquired Berkeley.

"**I'm** going to work to-morrow," replied Armstrong emphatically; "I'm going down to New York **to** enter **a** law office."

"**I** thought you **had** some notion of staying here and taking a course of graduate study."

"**No, sir!** The sooner **a** man gets into harness, **the better.** I've wasted enough time in **the** last four years. The longer a man loafs around in this old place, under pretense of reading and that kind of thing, the harder it is for him to take hold."

Armstrong was a rosy little man, with yellow hair and light eyes. His expression was one of irresolute good nature. His temper was sanguine and expansive, and he had been noted in college for anything but concentration of pursuit. **He** was gregarious in his habits, susceptible **tible** and subject to sudden enthusiasms. His good nature made him a victim to all the bores **and** idlers in the class, and his room became a favorite resort for men on their way to recitation, being on the ground floor and near the lecture rooms. They would drop it about half an hour before the bell rang, and make up a little game of "penny ante" around Armstrong's center table. In these diversions he seldom took part, as he had given it out publicly that he was

" studying for a stand "; but his abstinence from the game in no wise damped the spirits of his guests. Occasionally his presence would re- ceive the notice of the company somewhat as follows :

No. 1. " Make less noise, fellows; Charley is digging out that Puckle lesson."

No. 2. " You go into the bedroom, Charley, and shut the door, and then **you won't** be bothered by the racket."

No. 3. " **Oh,** hang the Puckle ! Come and **take** a hand, Charley. We'll let you in this pool without **an ante.**"

No. 4. " Why don't you get a new pack of cards, Charley ? **It's** a disgrace to you to keep such **a** dirty lot **of old** pasteboards for your friends."

In face of which abuse, Armstrong was as helpless as Telemachus under **the** visitation of the suitors. The resolute air with which he now declared his intention of grappling with life had therefore something comic about it, and Berkeley said, rather incredulously :

" I suppose you'll keep up your reading along with your law ? "

" **No,**" replied the other ; " Themis is a jeal- **ous** mistress. No; **I'm** going to bone right down to it."

" Haven't you changed your ideal **of life** lately ? " **asked** Clay a little scornfully,

" Perhaps I have," said Armstrong ; " per- haps I've had to."

" What *is* your ideal of life ? " I inquired.

"Well, I'll tell you," he answered, draining his coffee cup solemnly, and putting it down with the manner of a man who has made up his mind. The rest of us arranged ourselves in attitudes of attention. "My ideal is independence," began Armstrong. "I want to live my own life ; **and as** the first condition of independ-**ence is money, I'm** going **for** money. Culture **and taste,** and all that, are well enough when a **man** can afford it, but for a poor man it means **just so** many additional wants which he can't **gratify.** My father is an educated man ; a country minister with **a** small salary and a large family ; and his education, instead of being a blessing, has been an actual curse to him. He has pined for all sorts of things which he couldn't have—books, engravings, foreign travel, leisure for study, nice people, and nice things about him. I've made up my mind that, what-ever else I may be, I won't be poor, and I won't be a minister, and I won't have a wife and brats hanging to me. I tell you that, next to ill health, poverty is **the** worst thing that can happen to a man. All **the** sentimental griev-ances that are represented in novels and poetry **as** the deepest of human afflictions,—disap-pointed ambitions, death of friends, loss of faith, estrangements, having your girl go back on you,—they don't signify very long if a man has sound health and a full purse. The min-isters and novel writers and fellows that preach the sentimental view **of** life don't believe it themselves. It's a kind of professional or literary quackery with them. Just let them feel the pinch of poverty, and then offer them a higher salary or a chance to make a little ' sordid gain ' in some way, and see how quick they'll accept the call to 'a higher sphere of usefulness.' Berk, hand over a match, will you ; this cigar has gone out."

"Loud cries of ' We will—we will ' ! " said Berkeley. "But can it be? Has the poick turned cynic, and the sickly sentimentalist become a materialist and a misogynist ? "

(Armstrong was our class poet, and had worried the official muse on Presentation Day to the utterance of some four hundred lines filled with allusions to Alma Mater, Friendship's Altar, the Elms of Yale, etc. His piece on that occasion had been " pronounced, by a well known literary gentleman who was present, equal to the finest productions of our own Willis.")

"I'll bet the cigars," said Doddridge, "that Armstrong marries the first girl he sees in New York."

"Yes," said Clay, " his boarding-house keeper's daughter."

"And has a dozen children before he is forty," added Berkeley ; " a dozen kids, and all of them girls. Charley is sure to be a begetter of wenches."

"And writes birthday odes ' To My Infant Daughter ' for the *Home Journal,*" continued Clay.

"No, no," said the victim of this banter,

shaking **his head** solemnly. " I shall give no hostages to fortune. I mean to live snug and carry **as** little sail **as** possible : to leave only the narrowest margin out for Fate to tread on. The man who has the fewest exposed points leads, on the whole, the happiest life. How can **a** man enjoy himself freely when a piece of defective plumbing, the bursting of a toy pistol, the carelessness of a nurse, may plunge him into a lifelong sorrow ? I don't say it's a very noble life that I propose to myself, but it's a safe one. I'm too nervous and anxious to stand the responsibilities of matrimony."

" **If** you can't stand responsibility," said Doddridge, " I don't see why you choose the law for a profession. You don't seem to me cut out for a lawyer anyway. I always thought you meant **to** be some kind of a literary chap."

" Yes," said Berkeley, " why don't you go for **a** snug berth under the government, or study for a tutorship here ? That's the life that would suit you, old man."

" Not at all," answered Armstrong ; " I have a horror of any salaried position, or of any position where a man is obliged to conform his habits and opinions to other people's. It is the worst sort of dependence. Now a lawyer in successful practice, and especially if he is a bachelor, is about as independent as a man can be. His relations with his clients are merely professional, and what he does or thinks privately is nobody's business."

" If you are going to be a mere lawyer," asked Clay, " what becomes of your education and your intellectual satisfactions ? "

" A man can get his best intellectual satisfactions out of the work of his profession," answered Armstrong. " Besides, as to that, there's time enough. Fifteen years of solid work will enable one to put by a fair competence, if he lives carefully and has no one but himself to support ; and then he will be free to take up a hobby. Oh, I shall cultivate a hobby or two after a while. It keeps the mind healthy to have some interest of the kind outside of one's business. I may take to book-collecting or numismatics or raising orchids. Perhaps I may become an authority on ancient armor ; time enough for that by and by. And then I can cut over to Europe every summer if I like, and no one to interfere with my down-sittings or up-risings, my goings-out or my comings-in. Do you know," he went on, after a pause, " how I always look to myself in the glass of the future ? I figure myself like old Tulkinghorn, in ' Bleak House,'—going down into his reverberating vaults for a bottle of choice vintage, after the work of the day, and then sitting quietly in the twilight in his dusky, old-fashioned law chambers, sipping his wine while the room fills with the fragrance of southern grapes. The gay old silver-top ! "

There was silence for a few minutes after Armstrong had finished his declaration. It was broken by Berkeley, who had risen, and was

walking up and down in front of the fountain
with his hands thrust into his pockets.

"You couldn't lead that sort of life if you
tried," he said ; "you aren't built for it."

"Don't you make any mistake," rejoined the
other ; "it's the sort of life I'm going to live."

"**It's a** cowardly life," retorted Berkeley.

"**Did I** say **it** wasn't ? **I** said it was safe.
You can call it what you like."

"Well," replied Berkeley, reseating himself
again, "my ideal career is just the opposite of
that."

"Suppose you explain yours, then," said
Armstrong.

Berkeley hesitated a few moments before beginning. He was a lean, tallish fellow, with a
Scotch cast of countenance, **a** small blue eye,
high cheek bones, **a** freckled skin, and whity-
brown hair. **He** had a dry, cautious humor,
fed by much **out** of the way reading. He had
been distinguished in college by methodical
habits, a want of ambition, a disposition to keep
to himself, and **a** mixture of selfishness and
bonhomie which made him a cold friend but an
agreeable companion. It was therefore with
some surprise that we heard him deliver himself
as follows :

"I believe that the greatest mistake a man
can make is in not getting enough out of life.
I want to lead a full life, to have a wide experience, to develop my whole nature to the
utmost, to touch mankind at the largest
possible number of points. I want adventure,

change, excitement, emotion, suffering even
—l don't care what, so long as it is not stag-
nation. Just consider what there is on this
planet to be seen, learned, enjoyed, and what a
miserably small share of it most people appropriate. Why, there are men in my village who
have never been outside the county and seldom
out of the township ; who have never heard a
word of any language but English ; never seen
a city or a mountain or the ocean — or, indeed,
any body of water bigger than Fresh Pond or
the Hogganum River ; never been in a theater,
steamboat, library, or Cathedral. Cathedral !
Their conception of a church is limited to the
white wooden meeting-house at 'the center.'
Their art-gallery is the wagon of a traveling
photographer. Their metropolitan hotel is the
stoop and barroom of the 'Uncas House.'
Their university is the unpainted schoolhouse
on the hill. Their literature is the weekly newspaper from the county town. But take the
majority of educated men even. What a rusty,
small kind of existence they lead ! They are in
a rut, just the same as the others, only the rut
is a trifle wider. If I had my way I would
never do the same work or talk with the same
people — hardly live in the same place for two
days running. Life is too short to do a thing
twice. When I come to the end of mine I don't
want to say *J'ai manqué la vie* ; but make my
brag, with the Wife of Bath :

" ' Unto this day it doth myn herte bote
   That I have had my world as in my time.' "

" Well, how are you going to do all those
fine things ? " inquired Armstrong. " For instance, that about not living in one place two
days running. I'm afraid you'll find that in-
convenient, not to say expensive."

"Oh, you mustn't take me too literally. I may
have to travel on foot or take a steerage passage, but I shall keep going all the same. I
haven't made any definite plans yet. I shall
probably strike for something in the diplomatic
line—secretary **of** legation, or some small con-
sulship perhaps. But the principle is the main
thing, and the principle is : Don't do anything
because it's the nearest and easiest and most
obvious thing to do, but make up your mind to
get the best. Look at the lazy way in which
men accept their circumstances. There is the
matter of acquaintance, for instance—we let
chance determine it. We know the men that
we can't help knowing—the ones in the next
house, cousins and second cousins, business
connections, etc. Here at college, now, we get
acquainted with the fellows at the eating club
or in the same society, or those who happen to
sit next us in the classroom, because their
names begin with the same letter. That's
it ; it's just a sample of our whole life.
Our friendships, like everything else about
us, are determined by the alphabet. We go
with the Z's because some arbitrary system
of classification has put us among them,
instead of fighting our way up to the
A's, where we naturally belong. The conse-

quence is that **one's friends are mostly dreadful** bores."

" I'm sure we are all much **obliged to you**," murmured Clay parenthetically.

" **There are** about **two or** three **thousand** people in the world," continued Berkeley, " **su-** premely worth knowing. Why shouldn't *I* know them ? I will ! **Everybody** knows two or three thousand people—mostly very stupid people—or, rather, **he lets** them know **him.** Why shouldn't he use some choice in the matter ? Why **not** know Thackeray and Car- lyle, Lord Palmerston and the Pope, and the Emperor of China and all the great statesmen, authors, African explorers, military com- manders, artists, hereditary nobles, actresses, wits and belles of the best society, instead **of** putting **up** with Tom, Dick, and Harry ? "

" Berkeley, ' with whom the bell-mouthed flask had wrought ! ' " exclaimed Clay. " De- cidedly, Berk, you should take your coffee without cognac."

" Let me suggest," put **in** Doddridge, " that some of those parties you mentioned are not so easy to get introductions **to**."

"Oh, I say again, you **mustn**'t take me too literally. But even the **top s**wells are easier to know than you think. **All** that is wanted is a little cheek. But take it **in** a smaller way ; say that **we resolve to** cultivate the best society within our reach. Doubtless there are numbers of interesting and distinguished people right here in New Haven whose acquaintance it would be worth while to have. **But** how long would you beggars **live** here without making the least effort to look them out, and meanwhile put up with the same old everyday bores—like me, or Polisson here? And it's the same way with marriage. A fellow blunders into matri-**mony** with the first attractive girl that gives him the opportunity. He knows, if he takes the **time** to think about it, that there are a thousand others better than she, if he will wait and look through the world a little. 'Juxta-position in fine,' as Clough says."

" Of course, with such a brilliant destiny before you, *you'll* never marry," said I.

" Yes, I think I shall. I fancy that the noblest possibilities of life are never realized without marriage. Yes, I can think of nothing finer than to have **a** lot of manly boys and sweet girls growing up around one. But when **I** marry it shall be so as to give completeness and expansion to life, not narrowness and dullness. I shall never marry and settle down. Settle down ! What a damnable expression that is ! A man ought to settle *up*. I mean to have my fling first, too. I should like to gamble a bit at Baden-Baden. I should like to go out to Colo-rado and have a lick at mining speculations. I want to rough it some too, and see how life is lived close to the bone : ship for a voyage before the mast ; enlist for **a** campaign or two some-where and have joy of battle ; join the gypsies or the Mormons or the Shakers for a while, and taste all the queerness of things. And then I

want to float for another while **on the very top-**
most crest of society. I **want to** fight a duel
or two, elope with **a** marquise, do **a** little **of**
everything for **the** experience's sake, as a man
ought to take opium once in his life just **to**
know how **it** feels."

Whether **it** was indeed the cognac, **or** only
the unusual excitement attending this outburst
of pent-up fire, Berkeley's cheek had got a flush
upon it. Perhaps, too, **it** was **owing to the in-**
fluences of the day and the hour, the splash of
the **fountain, the** rustle **of** the vine-leaves, and
the wavering shadows which played about the
courtyard as the gas-jets flickered in the breeze
of night, that made his boastful words seem less
extravagantly out of character than they otherwise would. The silence which followed **his.**
speech was broken by Clay, who sat with his
foot on the rim of the fountain, balancing on
the hind legs of his chair, and looking thoughtfully **at** the slender jet as it rose and fell. He
still wore the dress suit in which he had figured
on the Commencement platform in the afternoon, and which set off the aristocratic grace
of his slight figure. There was a pale intellectual light in his face, and his black eyes had the
glow of genius.

" I think," he began, **" that** Berkeley makes a
mistake in confounding a full life with a restless one. I believe in a full experience too, but
the satisfactions should be inward ones. Take
the matter of foreign travel, for one thing, on
which you lay so much stress. It is a great

stimulus to the imagination, no doubt; but then foreign countries are accessible to the imagination by other means—through books and art, for example. I think **it** likely that the reality is, quite as often as not, disappointing. Place, after all, is indifferent. 'The soul is its own place'; you can't get rid of yourself by going abroad, and it's himself that a man gets sooner tired of than of anything else. Then as to acquaintances, I don't know that I should care to know personally such men as Thackeray and Carlyle, and the big composers and artists and other people **that** you mentioned. It might be equally disenchanting. They put the best of themselves into their books, or pictures, or music. I certainly would not seek their society through a formal introduction, at all events. It is hard for **a** small man to keep his self-respect in face of a great man when he obtains his acquaintance as a special favor. **If I** could meet some of those fellows, quite naturally and accidentally, on equal terms, **I** might like it, but not otherwise. But, leaving that point out of account, I think that the career which Berkeley proposes to himself would turn out very hollow. It would result in the superficial gratification of the curiosity and the senses ; and, as soon as the novelty got rubbed off, what is there left ? "

"So then,"said Berkeley, "you've swung into line with Armstrong, have you ? You mean to plod along in some professional rut too. What has got into all our idealists?"

"Not **by** any means," answered Clay. "Armstrong talks about independence, and yet destines himself to the worst kind of dependence — slavery to money-getting. Most people, it seems to me, spend the best part of their lives not in living, but in getting the means to live. We'll give Armstrong, say twenty years, to lay up enough money to retire on and begin to live. What sort of a position will he be in then to enjoy his independence ? His nature will have got so subdued to what it works in that the only safety for him will be to keep on at the law."

"All right ! Then I'll keep on," interjected Armstrong.

"What the devil do *you* mean to do then ?" asked Berkeley of Clay.

"I don't quite know yet," replied the latter. "I shall 'loaf and invite my soul' whenever I feel like it. I shall live as I go along, and not postpone it till I am forty. I shan't put myself into any mill that will grind me just so much a day. I need my leisure too badly for that. I presume I shall spend most of my time at first in reading and walking. Then, whenever I think of anything to write I shall write it, and if I can sell what I write to some publisher or other so much the better. If not, go on as before."

"Meanwhile, where will your bread and butter come from ?" asked Armstrong.

"Oh, I shan't starve. I can get some sort of hack work—something that won't take much of my time, and which I can do with my left hand. But the great point, after all, is to make your wants simple; to live like an Arab, content with a few dates and a swallow from the gourd. 'Lessen your denominator;' it's easier than raising your numerator, and the quotient is the same."

"**No, it's not** the same," Berkeley retorted. "Renunciation and enjoyment are not the same. **It** makes a heap of difference whether you have a thing or simply do without it. The plain living and high thinking philosophy may do for Clay, **whose** mind to him a kingdom is; but a fellow like me, whose mind is only a small Central American republic, can't live on the revenues of the spirit. The fact is, Clay, you've read too much Emerson. I went into that myself once, but **I** soon found out that it wouldn't wear. I want mine thicker. The worst thing about the career of a literary man or an artist is that, if he fails, there are no compensations; and success is mighty uncertain. Nobody doubts that you are smart enough, Clay, and I am sure we expect great things of you, whatever line you take up. But, for the sake **of** the argument, suppose you have grubbed along in a small way, living on crusts and water till you are fifty, without doing any really good work. Then where are you? You haven't had any fun. You've no other string to your bow. You haven't that practical experience of the world which would enable you to turn your hand to something else. You have no influence or reputation; for, of all poor things, poor art

of any kind is the worst—hateful to gods and
men and columns. In short, where are you?
You're out of the dance ; you don't count."

"Yes," added Armstrong, "and you've no
professional success or solid standing in the
community ; and, what's worse, you've no
money, which might make up for the want of
all the rest."

"I don't think you get my meaning. I may
fail," said Clay proudly ; "I may never even try
to succeed, in your sense of the word. I decline all mean competitions and all low views of
success. The noblest ideal of life—at least, the
noblest to me—is self-culture in the high meaning of the word ; the harmonious development
of one's whole nature. Armstrong has drawn a
picture of his future in the likeness of old Tulkinghorn. I suppose we are all accustomed to
put our anticipations into some such concrete
shape before our mind's eye. The typical situation which I am fond of imagining is something like this : I like to fancy myself sitting in
a dark old upper room of some remote farmhouse at the close of a winter day, after three
or four hours of steady reading or writing.
The room is full of books—the *best* books.
There is a little fire on the hearth, there is a
dingy curtain at the window. It is solitary and
still, and when the light gets too scant to let
me read any more, I fill my pipe and go and
stand in the window. Outside, there is a row
of leafless elms, and beyond that a dim wide
landscape of lakes and hills, and beyond that a

red, windy sunset. I can sit in that window and smoke my pipe and have my own thoughts till the hills grow black. There is no one to say to me ' Go ' or ' Come '; no patient **to** visit; no confounded case on the docket next morning at nine; **no** distasteful, mean, slavish job of any kind. How can I fail to have thoughts worth the thinking, and to live a rich and free life when I breathe every day the bracing **air** of nature and the great poets? Isn't such a life in itself the best kind of success, even if a man accomplishes nothing in particular that you can put your hand on?"

"Yes, I know," said Armstrong, taking a long breath. **"I** have felt that way, too. But a man has got to put all that sternly behind him and do the world's work for the world's wages, if he means to amount **to** anything. It's only a finer kind **of** self-indulgence, after all—egoistic hedonism and that sort of thing."

"It won't be all standing at windows and looking at sunsets," added Doddridge. "Has it ever occurred **to** you that, before entering on a life of self-denial and devotion to rather vague ideals, a man ought to be mighty sure of himself? Can you keep up the culture business without growing in on yourself unhealthily, and then getting sick of inaction? Don't you think there will be times of disappointment and doubt, when you look around and see fellows without half your talents getting ahead of you in the world?"

"Of course," answered Clay, " I shall have to make sacrifices, and I shall have to stick to them when made. But there have always been plenty of people willing to make similar sacrifices for similar compensations. Men have gone out into the wilderness or shut themselves up in the cloister for opportunities of study or self-communion, or for other objects which were perhaps at bottom no more truly devotional than mine. Nowadays such opportunities may be had by any man who will keep himself free from the servitude of a bread-winning profession. It is not necessary now to cry *Ecce in deserto* or *Ecce in penetralibus.* Oh, I shall have my dark days ; but whenever the blue devils get thick I shall take to the woods and return to sanity."

" You mean to live in the country, then ? " I inquired.

"Yes ; most of the time, at any rate. Nature is fully half of life to me."

Again there was a pause.

" Well, you next, Polisson," said Armstrong finally. " Let's hear what your programme is."

"Oh, nothing in the least interesting," I replied. " My future is all cut and dried. I shall spend the next two years in the south of France—mainly at Lyons—to learn the details of the silk manufacture. Then I shall come home to go into my father's store for a year, as a clerk in the importing department. At the close of that year the governor will take me in as junior partner, and I shall marry my second cousin. We shall live with my parents, and I am going to be very domestic, though, as

a matter of form, I shall join one or two clubs.
I shall go down town every morning at nine,
and come up at five."

"Quite a neat little destiny," said Armstrong.
"I wish I had your backing. Come, Dodd,
what's yours? You're the only man left."

"I haven't made up **my** mind yet," said
Doddridge slowly.

He was a large, spare man, with a swarthy
skin, a wide mouth, a dark, steady eye, and a
long jaw. There was an appearance of power
and will about him which was well borne
out by his character. He had been a system-
atic though not a laborious student, and while
maintaining a stand comfortably near the
head **of** the class, had taken **a** course in the
Law School during Senior year, doing his
double duties with apparent ease. He was a
constant speaker in the debates of the Linonian
Society, and the few who attended the meetings
of that moribund school of eloquence spoke of
Doddridge's speeches as oases in the waste
of forensic dispute, being always distinguished
by vigor and soundness, though without any
literary quality, such as Clay's occasional per-
formances had. Berkeley, who covered his
own lazy and miscellaneous reading with the
mask of eclecticism, and proclaimed his dis-
belief in a prescribed course of study, was wont
to say that Doddridge was the only man that
he knew who was using the opportunities
given by the college for all they were worth,
and really getting out of "the old curric" that

mental discipline which it professed to impart.
Though rather taciturn, he was not unsocial,
and was fond of his pipe in the evening. He
liked a joke, especially if it was of a definite
kind and at some one's expense, touching some
characteristic weakness of the man. There
was at bottom something a little hard about
him, though everyone agreed that he was a
good fellow. We all felt sure that he would
make a distinguished success in practical life;
and we doubtless thought—if we thought about
it at all—that, with his clear foresight and
habits of steady work, he had already decided
upon his career. His words were therefore a
surprise.

"What! you don't mean to say that you are
going to drift, Dodd?" inquired Armstrong.

"Drift? Well, no; not exactly. I shall
keep my steering apparatus well in hand, but
I haven't decided yet what port to run for.
There's no hurry. I have an uncle in the
Northwest in the lumber business who would
give me a chance. I may go out there and
look about a while at first. If it doesn't promise
much, there is the law to fall back upon. My
father has a fruit farm at Byzantium in Western
New York—where I come from, you know—
and he is part owner of the Byzantium weekly
Bugle. I've no doubt I could get on as editor
and go to the legislature. Or I might do worse
than begin on the farm; farming is looking up
in that section. I may try several things till I
find the right one."

" That's queer," said Armstrong. " I thought
you had made up your mind to enter the
Columbia Law School."

"Hardly," answered Doddridge, "though I
may, after all. The main point is to keep yourself in readiness for any work, and take the best
thing that turns up—like Berkeley here," he
added dryly.

Armstrong looked at his watch and remarked
that it was nearly midnight.

" Boys," said I, " **in** fifteen years from to-
night let's have a supper here and see how each
man of us has worked **out** his theory of life,
and how he likes it as far as he has got."

" Oh, give us twenty," said Doddridge, laughing, as we all arose and prepared to break up.
" No one accomplishes anything in this latitude
before he is forty."

.   .   .   .   .

It was in effect just fifteen years **from** the
summer of our graduation that I started out to
look up systematically my quondam classmates
and compare notes with them. The course of
my own life had been quite other than I had
planned. For one thing, I had lived in New
Orleans and not in New York, and my occasions
had led me seldom to the North. The first
visit I paid was to Berkeley. I had heard that
he was still unmarried, and that he had been for
years settled, as minister, over **a** small Episcopal parish on the Hudson. The steamer landed
me one summer afternoon at a little dock on
the west bank, and after obtaining from the

dock-keeper precise directions for finding the parsonage, I set out on foot. After a walk of a mile along a road skirted by handsome country seats, but contrasting strangely in its loneliness with the broad thoroughfare of the river constantly occupied by long tows of barges and rafts, I came to the rectory gate. The house was a stone cottage, covered with trailers, and standing well back from the road. In the same inclosure, surrounded by a grove of firs, was a little stone chapel with high pitched roof and rustic belfry. In front of the house I spied a figure which I recognized as Berkeley. He was in his shirt sleeves, and was pecking away with a hoe at the gravel walk, whistling meanwhile his old favorite " Bonny Doon." He turned as I came up the driveway, and regarded me at first without recognition. He, for his part, was little changed by time. There was the same tall, narrow-shouldered, slightly stooping figure ; the face, smooth-shaved, with a spot of wintry red in the cheek, and the old humorous cast in the small blue eyes.

" You don't know me from Adam," I said, pausing in front of him.

"Ah !" he exclaimed directly. " Polisson, old man, upon my conscience I'm glad to see you, but I didn't know you till you spoke. You've been having the yellow fever, haven't you ? Come in—come into the house."

We passed in through the porch, which was covered with sweet-pea vines trained on strings, and entered the library, where Berkeley resumed his coat. The room was lined with bookshelves loaded to the ceiling, while piles of literature had overflowed the cases and stood about on the floor in bachelor freedom. After the first greetings and inquiries, Berkeley carried my valise upstairs, and then returning, said :

"I'm a methodical though not methodistical person, or rather parson (excuse the Fullerism) ; and as you have got to stay with me until I let you go, that is, several days at the least (don't interrupt), I'll keep a little appointment for the next hour, if you will excuse me. A boy comes three times a week to blow the bellows for my organ practice. Perhaps you would like to step into the church and hear me."

I assented, and we went out into the yard and found the boy already waiting in the church porch. Berkeley and his assistant climbed into the organ loft, while I seated myself in the chancel to listen. The instrument was small but sweet, and Berkeley really played very well. The interior of the little church was plain to bareness ; but the sun, which had fallen low, threw red lights on the upper parts of the undecorated walls, and rich shadows darkened the lower half. Through the white, pointed windows I saw the trembling branches of the firs. I had been hurrying for a fortnight past over heated railways, treading fiery pavements, and lodging in redhot city hotels. But now the music and the day's decline filled me with a sense of religious calm, and for a moment I envied Berkeley.

After his practicing was over, the organist locked the chapel door, and we paced up and down in the fir grove on the matting of dark red needles, and watched the river, whose eastern half still shone in the evening light. After supper we sat out on the piazza, which commanded a view of the Hudson. Berkeley opened a bottle of Chablis, and produced some very old and dry Manilla cheroots, and, leaning back in our willow chairs, we proceeded to " talk Cosmos."

" You are very comfortably fixed here," I began ; " but this is not precisely what I expected to find you doing, after your declaration of principles, fifteen years ago, you may remember, on our Commencement night."

" Fifteen years ! So it is — so it is," he answered, with a sigh. " Well, *l'homme* **propose**, *pose*, you know. I don't quite remember what it was that I said on that occasion : dreadful nonsense, no doubt. As Thackeray says, a boy *is* an ass. Whatever it was, it proceeded, I suppose, from some temporary mood rather than from any permanent conviction, though, to be sure, I slipped into this way of life almost by accident at first. But, being in, I have found it easy to continue. I am rather too apt, perhaps, to stay where I am put. I am a quietist by constitution." He paused, and I waited for him to enter upon a fuller and more formal apology. Finally he went on much as follows :

" Just after I left college I made application through some parties at Washington for a foreign consulate. While I was waiting for the application to **be** passed on (it was finally unsuccessful), I came up here to visit my uncle, who was the rector **of this** parish. He was a widower without any children, and the church was his hobby. It is a queer little affair, something like **the old** field-kirks or chapels of ease in some parts of England. **It** was built partly **by my** uncle and partly by **a** few New York families who have country places here, and **who** use it in the summer. This is all glebe land," he said, indicating, with a sweep of his hand, the twilight fields below the house, sloping down toward the faintly glimmering river. "My uncle had a **sort** of prescription or lien by courtesy on the place. There's not much salary to speak of, but he had a nice plum of his own, and lived inexpensively. Well, that first summer I moped about here, got acquainted with **the** summer residents, read a good deal of the time, took long walks into the interior—a rough, aboriginal country, where **they** still talk Dutch—and waited for an answer **to my** application. When it came at last, **I** fretted about it considerably, and was for starting off in search of something else. I had an idea of getting a place as botanist on Coprolite's survey of the Nth parallel, and I wrote to New Haven for letters. I thought it would be a good outdoor, horseback sort of life, and might lead to something better. But that fell through, and meanwhile the dominie kept saying : 'My dear fellow, don't be in too much of a hurry to

begin. Young America goes so fast nowadays
that it is like the dog in the hunting story—a
leetle bit ahead of the hare. Why not stay here
for a while and ripen—ripen?' The dominie
had a good library—all my old college favorites,
old Burton, old Fuller, and Browne, etc., and it
seemed the wisest course to follow his advice
for the present. But in the fall my uncle had
a slight stroke of paralysis, and really needed
my help for a while; so that what had been
a somewhat aimless life, considered as loafing,
became all at once a duty. At first he had
a theological student, from somewhere across
the river, come to stay in the house and read
service for him on Sundays. But he was a
ridiculous animal, whose main idea of a minister's duties was to intone the responses in a
sonorous manner. He used to practice this on
week days in his surplice, and I remember
especially the cadence with which he delivered
the sentence : 'Yea, like a broken *wall* shall
ye be and as a ruined *hedge.*'

 "He got the huckleberry, as we used to say
in college, on that particular text, and it has
stuck by me ever since. The dominie fired him
out after a fortnight, and one day said to me:
'Jack, why don't *you* study for orders and take
up the succession here? You are a bookworm,
and the life seems to be to your liking.' Of
course, I declined very vigorously in the beginning, though offering to stay on so long as the
dominie needed my help. I used to do lay
reading on Sundays when he was too feeble.

Gradually, ' the idea of the life did sweetly creep into my study of imagination.' The quaintness of the place appealed to me. And here was a future all cut out for me ; no preliminary struggle, no contact with vulgar people, no cutthroat competition, but everything gentlemanly and independent about it. I had strong doubts touching my theology, and used to discuss them with my uncle, but he said—and said rightly, I now think—' You young fellows in college fancy that it's a mighty fine, bold thing to affect radicalism and atheism, and the Lord knows what all ; but it won't stick by you when you get older. Experience will soften your heart, and you'll find after a while that belief and doubt are not matters of the pure reason, but of the will. It is a question of *attitude*. Besides, the church is broad enough to cover a good many private differences in opinion. It isn't as if you were going to be a blue-nosed Presbyterian. You can stay here and make your studies with me, instead of going into a seminary, and when you are ready to go before the bishop I'll see that you get the right sendoff.' In short, here I am ! My uncle died two years after, when I was already in orders, and I've been here ever since."

" I should think you would get lonely sometimes, and make a strike for a city parish," I suggested.

" Why—no, I don't think I should care for ordinary parish work. The beauty of my position here is its uniqueness. In winter I keep

the church open for the aborigines till they get
snowed up and stop coming, and then I put
down to New York for about a month or two
of work at the Astor Library. Last winter I
held service for two Sundays running with one
boy for congregation. Finally I announced to
him that the church would be closed until
spring.

"What in the—— Well, what do you find to
do all alone up here?"

"Oh, there's always plenty to do, if you'll
only do it. I've been cultivating some virtuosi-
ties, among other things. Remind me to show
you my etchings when we go in. Did you
notice, perhaps, that little head over the table,
on the north wall? No? Then I smatter
botany some. I'll let you look over my *hortus
siccus* before you go. It has some very rare
ferns; one of them is a new species, and Fos-
ter—who exchanges with me—swore he was
going to have it named after me. I sent the
first specimen to have it described in his forth-
coming report. But doubtless all this sort of
thing is a bore to you. Well, lately I have been
going into genealogy, and I find it more and
more absorbing. Those piles of blank books
and manuscripts on the floor at the south end
are all crammed with genealogical notes and
material."

"I should think you would find it pretty dry
fodder," I said.

"That is because you take an outside, un-
sympathetic view of it. Now, to an amateur it's

anything but dry. There is as much excitement
in hunting down a missing link in a pedigree
that you have been on the trail of for a long
time, as there is in the chase of any other kind
of game."

"Do you ever get across the water? Travel,
if I remember right, played a large part in your
scheme of life once."

"Yes; I've been over once, for a few
months. But my income, though very com-
fortable for the statics of existence, is rather
short for the dynamics, and so I mostly stay
at home."

"Did you meet any interesting people over
there? Any of the crowned heads, famous
wits, etc., whom you once proposed to cultivate?"

"No; nobody in particular. I went in a very
quiet way. I had some good letters to people
in England, but I didn't present them. The
idea of introductions became a bore as I got
nearer to it."

"And, of course you didn't elope with the
marquise?"

"Was that in my scheme? Well, no, I did
not."

"You might have done worse, old man. You
ought to have a wife, to keep you from getting
rusty up here. And, besides, a fellow that goes
so much into genealogy should take some
interest in posterity. You ought to cultivate
the science practically."

"Oh, I'm past all danger of matrimony now,"

said Berkeley, with a laugh. "There was a girl that I was rather sweet on a few years ago. I was looking up a pedigree for her papa, and I found that I was related to her myself, in eight different ways, though none of them very near. I explained it to her one evening. It took me an hour to do it, and I fancy she thought it a little slow. At all events, when I afterward hinted that we might make the eight ways nine, she answered that our relationship was so intricate already that she couldn't think of complicating it any further. No, you may put me down as safe."

After this, we sat listening in silence to the distant beat of paddle-wheels where a steamer was moving up river.

"The river is a deal of company," resumed my host. "Thirty-six steamers pass here every twenty-four hours. That now is the *Mary Powell.*"

"Well," I said, answering not so much to his last remark as to the whole trend of his autobiography, "I suppose you are happy in this way of life, since you seem to prefer it. But it would be terribly monotonous to me."

"Happy?" replied Berkeley doubtfully. "I don't know. Happiness is a subjective matter. You *are* happy if you think yourself so. As for me, I cultivate an obsolete mood—the old-fashioned humor of melancholy. I don't suppose now that a light-hearted, French kind of chap like you can understand, in the least, what those fine, crusty old Elizabethans meant when they wrote,

> ' There's naught in this life sweet,
> If man were wise to see't,
> But only melancholy.'

This noisy generation has lost their secret.   As for me, I am content with the grays and drabs. I think the brighter colors would disturb my mood.   I know it's not a large life, but it is a safe one."

I did not at the moment remember that this had been Armstrong's very saying fifteen years ago, but some unconscious association led me to mention him.

"Armstrong and you have changed places in one respect, I should think," said I.   "He is keeping a boarding-school somewhere in Connecticut.   And instead of leading a Tulkinghorny existence in the New York University building, as he firmly intended, he has married and produced a numerous offspring, I hear."

"Yes, poor fellow!" said Berkeley; "I fancy that he is dreadfully overrun and hard up. There always was something absurdly domestic about Armstrong.   They say he has grown red, fat, and bald.   Think of a man with Armstrong's education—and he had some talent, too—keeping a sort of Dotheboys Hall!   I haven't seen him for eight or nine years.   The last time was at Jersey City, and I had just time to shake hands with him.   He was with a lot of other pedagogues, all going up to a teacher's

convention, or some such dreary thing, at
Albany."

I had an opportunity for verifying Berkeley's
account of Armstrong a few days after my conversation with the former. The Pestalozzian
Institute, in the pleasant little village of Thim-
bleville, was situated, as its prospectus informed
the public, on " one of the most elegant residence streets, in one of the healthiest and most
beautiful rural towns of Eastern Connecticut."
Over the entrance gate was a Roman arch bearing the inscription " Pestalozzian Institute " in
large gilt letters. The temple of learning itself
was a big, bare, white house at some distance
from the street, with an orchard and kitchen
garden on one side, and a roomy playground
on the other. The latter was in possession of
some small boys, who were kicking a broken-
winded football about the field with an amount
of noise greatly in excess of its occasion. To
my question where I could find Mr. Armstrong,
they answered eagerly : " Mr. Armstrong ?
Yes, sir. You go right into the hall, and knock
on the first door to the right, and he'll come—
or some one."

The door to the large square entry stood wide
open, and through another door opposite, which
was ajar, I saw long tables, and heard the clat-
ter of dishes being removed, while a strong
smell of dinner filled the air. I knocked at the
door on the right, but no one appeared. Finally,
a chubby girl of about ten summers came running round the corner of the house and into the

front door. She was eating an apple, and gazed at me wonderingly.

"Is Mr. Armstrong in?" I asked.

"Yes, sir; **he's** about somewhere. Walk into the parlor, please, and sit down, and I'll find him."

I entered the room on the right, which was **a** bleak and official-looking apartment,—apparently the reception room where parents held interviews with the instructor of youth, or tore themselves from the parting embraces of home-sick sons at **the** beginning of a new term. There is always something depressing about the parlor of an "institution" of any kind, and I could not help feeling sorry for Armstong, as I waited for him, seated on a sofa covered with faded rep. At length the door of an inner room opened, and the principal of the Pestalozzian Institute waddled across the floor with his hand held out, crying :

"Franky Polisson, how are you?"

He certainly had grown stout, and his light **hair** had retreated from the forehead. He wore glasses and was dressed in a suit of rusty black, with a high vest which gave him a ministerial look—a much more ministerial look than Berkeley had. His pantaloons presented that appearance which tailors describe as "kneeing out." He sat down, and we chatted for half an hour. The little girl had followed him into the room, and behind her came another three or four years her junior. The older one stood by his side, and he kept his arm around her, while he held the younger on his knee. They were both pretty, healthy-looking children, and kept their eyes fixed on " the man."

" Are those your own kids?" I inquired presently.

" Yes, two of them. I have six, you know," he answered, with a fond sigh ; " five girls and one boy. The lasses are rather in the majority."

" I heard you were quite a *paterfamilias,*" I said. " Won't you come and kiss me, little girl ? "

To this proposal the elder answered by bury- ing her head bashfully in her father's shoulder, while the smaller one simply opened her eyes wider and stared with more fixed intensity.

" Oh, by the way,". exclaimed Armstrong, " of course you'll take tea with us and spend the evening. I wish I could offer to sleep you here; but the fact is, Mrs. Armstrong's sister is with us for a few days, and the parents of one of my boys, who is sick, are also staying here ; so that my guest chambers are full."

" Don't mention it," I said. " I couldn't stay over night. I've got to be in New York in the morning, and must take the nine o'clock train. But I'll stay to supper and much obliged, if you are sure I shan't take up too much of your time."

" Not the least—not the least. This is a half holiday, and nothing in particular to do." He bustled to the door and called out loudly, " Mother ! Mother ! "

There was no response,

" **Nelly**," he commanded, " run and find your
mamma, and tell her that **Mr.** Polisson—from
New Orleans—an old classmate of papa's, will
be here to tea. That's a good girl. Polisson,
put on your hat and let's go round the place. I
want to show you what an establishment I've
got here."

We accordingly made the tour of the prem-
ises, Armstrong doing the cicerone impressively,
and every now and then urging me with emphatic hospitality to come and spend a week—a
fortnight—longer, if I chose, during the summer
vacation.

" Bring Mrs. Polisson and the kids. Bring
'em all," he said. " It will do them good ; the
air here is fine ; eleven hundred feet above the
sea. No malaria—no typhoid. I laid out four
hundred dollars last year on sewerage."

It being a half holiday, most of the big boys
had gone to a pond in the neighborhood for
a swim, under the conduct of the classical
master—a Yale graduate, Armstrong explained,
who had stood fourth in his class, " and a very
able fellow, very able."

But while we sat at tea in Armstrong's
family dining room, which adjoined the school
commons, we were made aware of the return
of the swimming party by the constant shuffle
and tramp of feet through the hall and the
noise of feeding in the next room. At our
table were present Mrs. Armstrong, her sister
(who had a frightened air when addressed and
conversed in monosyllables), the parents of the

sick pupil, and Armstrong's two eldest children. I surmised that the younger children had been in the habit of sharing in the social meal, and had been crowded out on this occasion by the number of guests; for I heard them *fremunting in carcere* behind a door through which the waitress passed out and in, bringing plates of waffles. The remonstrances of the waitress were also audible, and, when the wailing rose high, my hostess' face had a distrait expression, as of one prepared at any moment for an irruption of infant Goths.

Mrs. Armstrong was a vivacious little woman, who, I conjectured, had once been a village belle, with some pretensions to *espièglerie* and the fragile prettiness common among New England country girls. But the bearing and rearing of a family of children, and the matronizing of a houseful of hungry school-boys in such a way as to make ends meet, had substituted a faded and worried look for her natural liveliness of expression. She bore up bravely, however, against the embarrassments of the occasion. In particular, it pleased her to take a facetious view of college life.

"Oh, Mr. Polisson," she cried, "I am afraid that you and my husband were very gay young men when you were at college together. Oh, don't tell me; I know—I know. I've heard of some of your scrapes."

I protested feebly against this impeachment, but Armstrong winked at me with the air of a sly dog, and said:

"It's no use, Polisson. You can't fool Mrs. A. Buckingham and one or two of the fellows have been here to dinner occasionally, and I'm afraid they've given us away."

"Yes," she affirmed, "Mr. Buckingham was one of you, **too, I** guess, though he *is* the Rev. Mr. Buckingham now. Oh, he has told me."

"You remember old Buck?" put in Armstrong. "He is preaching near here—settled over a church at Bobtown."

"Yes," I answered, "I remember there was such a man in the class, but really I didn't know that he was—ah—such a character as you seem to infer, Mrs. Armstrong."

"Oh, he has quieted down now, I assure you," said the lady. "**He** is as prim and proper as a Methodist meeting-house. Why, he *has* to be, you know."

This amusing fiction of the wildness of Armstrong's youth had evidently become a family tradition and even, by **a** familiar process, an article of belief in his own mind. It reminded me grotesquely of Justice Shallow's reminiscences with Sir John Falstaff: "Ha, Cousin Silence, that thou hadst seen that, that this knight and I have seen. . . Jesu, Jesu, the mad days that I have spent!"

The resemblance became still stronger when, as we rose from the table, the good fellow beckoned me into a closet which opened off the dining room, saying, in **a** hoarse whisper:

"Here, Polisson, come in here."

He was uncorking a large bottle half filled

with some red liquid, **and as** he poured a por-
tion of this into **two** glasses he explained:

"I don't have this sort of thing on the table,
you understand, on account of the children and
my—ah—position. **It** would make talk. But
I tell you this is some of the real old stuff.
How!" And he held his glass up to the light,
regarding it with the one eye **of** a connoisseur,
and then drank down its contents with a smack.
I **was** considerably astonished, on doing the
same, to discover that this dark beverage—
which, from Armstrong's manner, I had been
prepared **to** find something at least as wicked as
absinthe—was simply and solely Bordeaux of a
mild quality. After this Bacchanalian proceed-
ing we went out into the orchard, which was
reserved for family use, and sat **on** a bench
under **an apple** tree. Armstrong called his
little boy who had been at supper with us and
gave him a whispered message, together **with**
some small change. The messenger disappeared, and after a short absence returned with
two very domestic cigars, transparently bought
for the nonce from some neighboring grocer.

"Have a smoke," commanded my host, and we
solemnly kindled the rolls **of** yellow leaf, Armstrong puffing away **at his** with the air of a
man who, though intrusted by destiny with the
responsibility of molding the characters of
youth, has not forgotten how to be a man of
the world on occasion.

"Well, Charley," I began, after a few preliminary draughts, **" you** seem to have a good

thing of it.   Your school is prosperous, I **under**-
stand; the work suits you; you have a mighty
pretty family of children growing **up,** and your
health appears to be perfect."

"Yes," he admitted; "I suppose I ought to
be thankful. I certainly enjoy great mercies.
It's **a** warm, crowded kind of life; plenty of
affection—plenty of anxiety too, to be sure.
I like **to** have the boys around me; it keeps
one's heart fresh, though in a way it's sometimes wearing to the nerves. Yes, I like the
young rascals—I like them. But, of course, it
has its drawbacks. Most careers have," he
added, in a burst of commonplace.

"It is not exactly the career that you had cut
out for yourself," I suggested, "when we talked
our plans over, you remember, that last evening
at New Haven."

"No, it's not," he acknowledged; "but perhaps it is a better one. What was it I said
then? I really don't recall it. Something very
silly, no doubt."

"Oh, **you** said, in a general way, that you
were going in for money and celibacy and selfishness—just as you have *not* done."

"Yes, yes; I know, I remember now," he
said, laughing. "Boys are great fools with
their brag of what they are going to do and be.
Life knocks it out of them fast enough; they
learn to do what they must."

"Do you ever write any poetry nowadays?"

"No, no; not I. The muse has given me
the go-by completely. Except **for** some occa-

sional verses for a school festival or something of the kind, which I grind out now and then, I've sunk my rhyming dictionary deeper than ever plummet sounded. The chief disadvantage of running a big school like this," he continued, with a sigh, "is the want of leisure and retirement to enable a man to keep up his studies. Sometimes I actually ache for solitude —for a few weeks or months of absolute loneliness and silence. Mrs. Armstrong has fixed me up a nice little private study—remind me to take you in there before you go—where I keep my books, etc. But the children will find their way in, and then I'm seldom undisturbed anywhere for more than an hour at a time; there's always some call on me—something wanted that no one else can see to."

"You ought to swap places with Berkeley for a while. He's got more leisure than he knows what to do with."

"Berkeley! Well, what's he up to now? Philately? Arboriculture? What's his last fad? You've seen him lately, you said. I met him for a minute in New York, a few years ago, and he told me he was going to an old book auction."

"He's got genealogy at present," I explained.

"Genealogy! What hay! What sawdust! Aren't there enough live people to take an interest in, without grubbing up dead ones from tombstones and town clerks' records? Berkeley must be a regular old bachelor antiquary by this time, with all human sympathy dried out of him. **No, I** wouldn't change with *him.* Would we, fatty ? " he said, appealing to a small offspring of uncertain sex which had just toddled out the door and across the gang-way to kiss its papa good-night.

I took leave of Armstrong and his interesting family with **a** sense of increased liking. His unworldliness, good nature, and simple little enthusiasms and self-satisfactions had some-how kept him young, and he seemed quite the **old** Armstrong **of** college days. I afterward learned that the excellent fellow had just finished his law studies and was preparing to enter upon practice, when his father's health failed, forcing him to give **up his** parish, and leaving **a** number of younger brothers and sisters partly dependent on Armstrong. He had accordingly taken the first situation that promised a fair salary, and, having got started **upon** the work of teaching, had been unable to let go until it was too late ; had, indeed, got deeper **and** deeper in, by falling in love and impulsively marrying at the first opportunity, and finally setting up for himself at the Pesta-lozzian Institute. Poor fellow ! Good fellow ! *Amico mio, non della ventura.*

My next call was upon Clay, who had rooms in the Babel building in New York, and was reported to **be** something of a Bohemian. He received me in a smoking jacket and slippers. **He** had grown a full beard, which hid his finely cut features. His black eyes had the old

fire, but his skin was sallower, and I thought
that his manner had a touch of listlessness,
mingled with irritability and defiance. He was
glad to see me ; but inclined to be at first, not
precisely distant, yet by no means confidential,
After a while, however, he thawed out and
became more like the Clay whom I remembered—our college genius, the brilliant, the
admired, in those days of eager hero worship.
I told him of my visits to Berkeley and
Armstrong.

" Berkeley I see now and then in town," said
Clay. " It was rather queer of him to turn
parson, but I guess he doesn't let his theology
bother him much. He has a really superior
collection of etchings, I am told. Armstrong,
I haven't seen in years. I knew he was a peda-
gogue somewhere in Connecticut."

" Don't you ever go to the class reunions ? "
I asked.

" Class reunions ? Well, hardly."

" I should think you would ; you are so near
New Haven."

" How charmingly provincial you are—you
Southern chaps ! Don't you know that, to a
man who lives in New York, nothing is near?
Besides, as to my classmates at old Yale and
all that, I would go round a corner to avoid
meeting most of them."

I expressed myself as duly shocked by this
sentiment, and presently I inquired :

"Well, Clay, how are you getting on, anyway ? "

"That's a d——d general question.   How do you want me to answer it?"

"Oh, not at all, if you don't like."

"Well, don't get miffed.   Suppose I answer, 'Pretty well, I thank you, sir.'   How will that do?"

"Are you writing anything now?"

"I'm always scribbling something or other. At present I've got the position of dramatic critic on the *Daily Boreas*, which is not a very bad bore, and keeps the pot boiling.   And I do more or less work of a hack kind for the magazines and cyclopedias, etc."

"I thought you were on the *Weekly Prig*. Berkeley or somebody told me so."

"So I was at one time, but I got out of it. The work was drying me up too fast.   The concern is run by a lot of cusses who have failed in various branches of literature themselves, and undertake in consequence to make it unpleasant for everyone else who tries to write anything.   I got so that I could sling as cynical a quill as the rest of them.   But the trick is an easy one and hardly worth learning.   It's a great fraud, this business of reviewing.   Here's a man of learning, for instance, who has spent years of research on a particular work.   He has collected a large library, perhaps, on his subject; knows more about it than anyone else living.   Then along comes some insolent little whipper-snapper—like me—whose sole knowledge of the matter in hand is drawn from the very book that he pretends to criticise, and patronizes the learned author in a book **notice**. No, **I got out of it**; I hadn't the cheek."

"**I bought** your **book**," * said **I**, "**as** soon as it came out."

"That's more than the public **did**."

"**Yes, and** I read it, **too**."

"No! Did you, **now**? That's true friendship. Well, how did **you** like it? Did you **get** your money's worth?"

I hesitated **a moment** and then answered:

"It was clever, **of** course. Anything that you write would be sure to be that. But **it** didn't appear to get down **to** hard-pan or to take a firm grip on life—did it?"

"Ah, that's what the critics said—only they've got a set of phrases **for** expressing it. They said it was amateurish, that it was in **a** falsetto key, etc."

"Well, how does **it** strike you, yourself? You know that it didn't come out **of** the deep places of your nature, don't you? You feel that you've got better behind?"

"Oh, I don't know. **A** man does what he can. I rather think it's the best I can do at present."

"Why don't you go at some more serious work? **some** *magnum opus* that would bring your whole strength into play?"

"A *magnum opus*, my dear **fellow**!" replied **Clay**, with a shade of irritation in his voice.

* Dialogues and Romances. **By** E. Clay. New York: Pater & Sons, 1874.

"You talk as if a *magnum opus* could be done for the wishing. Why don't *you* do a *magnum opus*, then ?"

"Why don't *I ?* Oh, I'm not **a** literary fellow—never professed to be. What a question !"

"Well, no more am I, perhaps. I don't think **any better of** the stuff that I scribble than you **do.** It's all an experiment with me. I'm trying my brushes—trying my brushes. Perhaps I may be able to do something stronger some day, and perhaps not. But at all events I **shan't** force my mood. I shall wait for my inspiration. One thing I've noticed, that as a man grows older **he** loses his spontaneity and gets more critical with himself. I could do more, no doubt, **if I** would only let myself go. But I'm like this meerschaum here—a hard piece and slow in coloring."

"Well, meanwhile you might do something in the line of scholarship, a history or a volume of critical essays—' Hours with the Poets,' or something of that kind, that would bring in the results of your reading. Have you seen Brainard's book ? It seemed to me work that was worth doing. But you could do something of the same kind, only much better, without taking your hands out of your pockets."

Brainard was a painstaking classmate of ours, who had been for some years Professor of Mental and Moral Philosophy, English Literature, and European History, in a western university, and had recently published a volume entitled

" Theism and Pantheism in the Literature of the English Renaissance," which was well spoken of, and was already in its third edition.

"Yes, I've seen the stuff," said Clay. " My unhappy country swarms with that sort of thing: books about books, and books about other books about books—like the big fleas and little fleas. It's not literature; it's a parasitic growth that infests literature. I always say to myself, with the melancholy Jaques, whenever I have to look over a book by Brainard or any such fellow, 'I think of as many matters as he; but I give Heaven thanks and make no boast of them.' No, I don't care to add anything to that particular rubbish heap. You know Emerson said that the worse poem is better than the best criticism of it. The trouble with me is that what I want to do I can't do—at present; what I can do I don't think it worth while to do—worth my while, at least. Someone else may do it and get the credit and welcome."

"But you do a good deal of work that you don't care about, as it is," I objected.

"Of course. A man must live, and so I do the nearest thing and the one that pays quickest. I got eighty dollars, now, for that last screed in *The Reservoir*.

"But," I persisted, "I thought that money-making had no part in your scheme. You could make more money in a dozen other businesses."

"So I could," he answered; "but they all involve some form of slavery. Now, I am my own master. After all, every profession has its drudgery, and literary drudgery is not the worst."

"Well," I conceded, "independent **of** what you accomplish, I suppose your way **of** life furnishes as many daily satisfactions as any. I sometimes envy you and Berkeley your freedom from business cares and **your** opportunities for **study.** What becomes of most men's college training, **for** example? By Jove! I picked up a Greek book the other day, and I couldn't read **three words** running. Now, I take it, you manage to keep up **your** classics, among other things."

"Oh, my way of life has its compensations," he answered. "But Sidney Smith—wasn't it?—said that life was a middling affair, anyway. As for the classics, etc., I find that reading and study lose much of their stimulus unless they **get** an issue in action—unless one can apply **them** directly toward his own work. I often think that, if I were fifteen or even ten years younger, I would go into some branch of natural science. **A** scientific man always seems to me peculiarly happy in the healthy character of his work. He can keep himself apart from it. It is objective, impersonal, makes no demand on his emotions. Now a writing man has to put himself into his work. He has to keep looking out all the time for impressions, material; to keep trying to enlarge and deepen his own experience, and he gets self-conscious and loses his freshness in the process."

"I am surprised to find you in New York," said I, by way of changing the subject. "I thought you had laid out to live in the country. Do you remember that pretty little word-picture of a winter afternoon that you drew us—something in the style of an *Il Penseroso* landscape? I expected to find you domesticated in a Berkshire farmhouse."

"Yes, I remember. I tried it. But I find it necessary, for my work, to be in New York. The newspapers—confound 'em !—won't move into the woods. But, after all, place is indifferent. See here; this isn't bad."

He drew aside the window curtain, and I looked out over a wilderness of roofs to the North River and the Palisades tinged with a purple light. The ferryboats and tugs plying over the water in every direction, the noise of the steam whistles, and the clouds of white vapor floating on the clear air, made an inspiriting scene.

"I'm up among the architects here," continued Clay ; "nothing but the janitor's family between me and the roof."

We talked a while longer, and on taking leave I said :

"I shall be on the lookout for something big from you one of these days. You know what we always expected of you. So don't lose your grip, old man."

"Who knows ? " he replied. "It doesn't rest with me, but with the *daimon.*"

I was unable to visit Doddridge, the remaining member **of** our group. He lived in the thriving town of Wahee, Minnesota, and I had heard **of** him, in **a** general way, as highly prosperous. He was **a** prominent lawyer and successful politician, and had lately been appointed United States district judge, after representing his section in the state senate for **a** term or **two.** I wrote to him, congratulating him on his success and asking for details. I mentioned also my visits to Berkeley, Armstrong, and Clay. I got a prompt reply from Doddridge, from which I extract such portions as are material to this narrative :

The first few months after I left college, I traveled pretty extensively through the West, making contracts with the farmers, as agent for a nursery and seed farm in my part of the country, but really with the object of spying out the land and choosing a place to settle in. Finally I lit on Wahee, and made up my mind that it was a town with a future. It was bound **to** be a railroad center. **It** had a first-rate agricultural country around it and a rich timber region a little further back ; and it already had an enterprising little pop. growing rapidly. To-day Wahee is as smart a city of its inches as there is in the Northwest. I squatted right down here, got a little raise from the old man, and put it all into building lots. I made a good thing of it, and paid it all back in six years with eight per cent. interest. Meanwhile, I went into Judge Pratt's law office and made my salt by fitting his boy for college—till I learned enough law to earn a salary. The judge was an old Waheer—belonged to the time-honored aristocracy of the place, having been here at least

fifteen years before I came. He got into railroads
after a while (is president now of the Wahee and
Heliopolis Bee Line), and left his law practice to me.
I married his daughter Alice in 1875. She is a
Western girl, but she was educated at Vassar. We
have two boys. If you ever come out our way,
Polisson, you must put up with us for as long as you
can stay. I would like to show you the country
about here, and have you ride after my team. I've
got a pair that can do it inside three minutes. Do
you remember Liddell of our class? He is an
architect, you know. I got him to come to Wahee,
and he has all he can do, putting up business blocks.
We have got some here equal to anything in
Chicago. . . .

Yes, I am United States judge for this district.
There is not much money in it, but it will help me
professionally by and by. I shall not keep it long.
Do I go into politics much, you ask. I used to, but
I've got through for the present. The folks about
here wanted to run me for Congress last term, but I
hadn't any use for it. As to what you are kind
enough to say about my "success," etc., whatever
success I have had is owing to nothing but a capacity
for hard work, which is the only talent that I lay
claim to. They want a man out here who will do
the work that comes to hand, and keep on doing it
till something better turns up. . . .

So Berkeley has turned out a dilettante instead of
an African explorer. I heard he was a minister.
He does not seem to have much ambition even in
that line of life. I should think Armstrong had got
the right kind of place for him. He was a good fellow, but never had much practical ability. You say
very little about Clay. How is old "Sweetness and

Light," anyway ?   I saw some fluff of his in one of the
magazines—a " romance" I think he called it.   This
is not an age for scribbling romances.   The country
wants something solider.   I never took much stock in
philosophers like Berkeley and Clay.   There is the
the same thing **the** trouble with them both : they
don't want **to do** any hard work, and they conceal
their laziness under fine names—culture, transcen-
dentalism, **and** what not ? '' Feeble and restless
youths, born to inglorious days."

This letter may **be** supplemented by another
—say Exhibit B—which I received from Clay
not long after :

MY DEAR POLISSON :
    It occurs to me that your question the other day,
as to how I was '' getting on," did not receive as
candid an answer as **it** deserved.   I am afraid that
you carried away **an** impression of **me** as of a man
who suspected himself **to be a** failure, but had not
the manliness to acknowledge it.   You will **say,**
perhaps, that there are all degrees of half success
short **of** absolute failure.   But I say no.   In the career which **I** have chosen, to miss of success—pronounced, unquestionable success—is to fail ; and I
am not weak enough to hide from myself on which
side of the line I fall.   **The** line is a very distinct
one, after all.   The fact is, **I** took the wrong turning, and it is too late to go back.   I am a case of
arrested development—a common enough case.   I
might give plenty **of** excellent excuses to my friends
for not having accomplished what they expected me
to.   But the world doesn't want apologies ; if wants
performance.

You **will** think this letter a most extraordinary outburst **of** morbid vanity. **But** while I **can afford to** have you think me **a failure, I** couldn't let you **go on** thinking **me a** fraud. That must be my excuse for writing.

Yours, as ever,

E. CLAY.

This letter moved **me deeply** by its characteristic mingling of egotism and elevation of feeling. **As I held** it **open in my hand, and** thought over **my classmates' fortunes,** I was led to make **a** few reflections. From **the fact** that Armstrong and Berkeley **were** leading lives that squarely contradicted **their** announced ideals and intentions, it was an obvious, but **not** therefore a true, inference that circumstance is usually stronger than will. Say, rather, that **the** species **of necessity** which consists in character and inborn **tendency is stronger than** any resolution **to** run counter **to it.**

Both Armstrong **and** Berkeley, on our Commencement night, had spoken from a sense of their own limitations, and **in** violent momentary rebellion against them. **But,** in talking with them fifteen **years** later, **I** could not discover that the **lack of** correspondence between their ideal future **and** their actual present troubled **them** much. It **is** matter **of common** note **that it is** impossible **to** make one **man** realize another's experience; **but** it **is often quite as hard** to make him recover a past stage of his own consciousness.

These, then, **had bent to** the force of chance

or temperament.   But Clay had shaped his life according to his programme, and had the result been happier?   He who gets his wish often suffers a sharper disappointment than he who loses it.   "*So täuscht uns also bald die Hoff-nung, bald das Gehoffte*," says the great pes-simist, and Fate is never more ironical than when she humors our whim.   Doddridge alone, who had thrown himself confidingly into the arms of the Destinies, had obtained their capricious favors.

I cannot say that I drew any counsel, civil or moral, from these comparisons.   Life is deeper and wider than any particular lesson to be learned from it; and just when we think that we have at last guessed its best meanings, it laughs in our face with some paradox which turns our solution into a new riddle.

VI.

A GRAVEYARD IDYL.

VI.

A GRAVEYARD IDYL.

N the summer of 187-, when young Doctor Putnam was recovering from an attack of typhoid fever, he used to take short walks in the suburbs of the little provincial town where he lived. He was still weak enough to need a cane, and had to sit down now and then to rest. His favorite haunt was an old-fashioned cemetery lying at the western edge of the alluvial terrace on which the town is built. The steep hillside abuts boldly on the salt marsh. One of the cemetery paths runs along the brink of the hill; and here, on a wooden bench under a clump of red cedars, Putnam would sit for hours enjoying the listless mood of convalesence, where the will remains passive, the mind, like an idle weathercock, turns to every puff of suggestion, and the senses, born new from sickness, have the freshness and delicacy of a child's. It soothed his eye to follow lazily the undulations of the creek, lying like the folds of a blue silk ribbon on the flat ground of the marsh below. He watched the ebbing tide suck down the water from the even lines of trenches that sluiced the meadows, till the black mud at their bottom glistened in the sun.   The opposite hills were dark with the heavy foliage of July.   In the distance a sail or two speckled the flashing waters of the bay, and the lighthouse beyond bounded the southern horizon.

It was a quiet, shady old cemetery, not much disturbed by funerals.   Only at rare intervals a fresh heap **of** earth and a slab **of** clean marble intruded, with their tale of a new and clamorous grief, among the sunken mounds and weather-stained tombstones of the ancient sleepers for **whom** the tears had long been dried.   Now **and** then a mourner came **to** put flowers on a grave ; now and then one of the two or three laborers who kept the walks and shrubberies in order would come along the path by Putnam's bench, trundling a squeaking wheelbarrow ; sometimes a nurse with a baby-carriage found her way in.   But generally the only sounds to break the quiet were the songs of birds, the rumble of a wagon over the spile bridge across the creek and the whetting **of** scythes in the water-meadows, where the mowers, in boots up **to** their waists, went shearing the oozy plain and stacking up the salt hay.

One afternoon Putnam was in his accustomed seat, whistling softly to himself and cutting his initials into the edge of the bench. The air was breathless, and the sunshine lay so hot on the marshes that it seemed to draw up **in** a visible steam a briny incense which mingled with a spicy smell of the red cedars.

Absorbed in reverie, he failed to notice how
the scattered clouds that had been passing
across the sky all the afternoon were being
gradually re-enforced by big fluffy cumuli rolling
up from the north, until a rumble overhead and
the rustle of a shower in the trees aroused him.

In the center of the grounds was an ancient
summer-house standing amid a maze of flower
beds intersected by gravel walks. This was
the nearest shelter, and, as the rain began to
patter smartly, Putnam pocketed his knife,
turned up his coat collar, and ran for it. Arrived at the garden-house, he found there a
group of three persons, driven to harbor from
different parts of the cemetery. The shower
increased to a storm, the lattices were lashed
by the rain, and a steady stream poured from
the eaves. The althæa and snowberry bushes
in the flower-plots, and even the stunted box-
edges along the path, swayed in the wind. It
grew quite dark in the summer-house, shaded
by two or three old hemlocks, and it was only
by the lightning flashes that Putnam could
make out the features of the little company of
refugees. They stood in the middle of the
building, to avoid the sheets of rain blown in
at the doors in gusts, huddling around a pump
that was raised on a narrow stone platform—
not unlike the daughters of Priam clustered
about the great altar in the penetralia :

Præcipites atra ceu tempestate columbæ.

They consisted of a young girl, an elderly

woman with a trowel and watering-pot, **and a**
workman in overalls, who carried a spade and
had perhaps been interrupted in digging a grave.
The platform around the pump hardly gave
standing room for **a** fourth. Putnam accordingly took his seat on a tool chest near one of
the entrances, and, while the soft spray blew
through the lattices over his face and clothes,
he watched the effect of the lightning flashes
on the tossing, dripping trees of the cemetery
grounds.

Soon **a** shout was heard and down one of the
gravel walks, now a miniature river, rushed a
Newfoundland dog, followed by a second man
in overalls. Both reached shelter soaked and
lively. The dog distributed the contents of his
fur over the party by the pump, nosed inquir-
ingly about, and then subsided into **a** corner.
Second laborer exchanged **a** few words with
first laborer, and melted into the general silence.
The slight flurry caused by their arrival was
only momentary, while outside the storm rose
higher and inside it grew still darker. Now
and then someone said something in a low
tone, addressed rather to himself than to the
others, and lost in the noise of the thunder and
rain.

But **in** spite of the silence there seemed to
grow up out of the situation a feeling of intimacy between the members of the little community in the summer-house. The need of
shelter—one of the primitive needs of humanity
—had brought them naturally together and shut

them up "in a tumultuous privacy of storm." In a few minutes, when the shower should leave off, their paths would again diverge, but for the time being they were inmates and held a household relation to one another.

And so it came to pass that when it began to grow lighter and the rain stopped, and the sun glanced out again on the reeking earth and saturated foliage, conversation grew general.

"Gracious sakes!" said the woman with the trowel and watering-pot as she glanced along the winding canal that led out from the summer-house—"just see the water in them walks!"

"Gol! 'tis awful!" murmured the Irishman with the spade. "There'll be a fut of water in the grave, and the ould mon to be buried the morning!"

"Ah, they had a right to put off the funeral," said the other workman, "and not be giving the poor corp his death of cold."

"'Tis warrum enough there where the ould mon's gone, but 'tis cold working for a poor lad like mesilf in the bottom of a wet grave. Gol! 'tis like a dreen." With that he shouldered his spade and waded reluctantly away.

Second laborer paused to light his dhudeen, and then disappeared in the opposite direction, his Newfoundland taking quite naturally to the deepest puddles in their course.

"Hath this fellow no feeling of his business?" asked Putnam, rising and sauntering up to the pump. The question was meant more for the younger than the elder of the two

women, but the former paid no heed to it, and
the latter, by way of answer, merely glanced at
him suspiciously and said "H'm!" She was
unlocking the tool-chest on which he had been
sitting, and **now** raised the lid, stowed away
her trowel and watering-pot, locked the chest
again and put the key in her pocket with the
remark, "I guess I haint got any more use
for a sprinkle-pot to-day."

"It *would* be rather superfluous," said Putnam.

The old woman looked at him still more dis-
trustfully, **and** then, drawing up her skirts,
showed **to** his great astonishment a pair of
india-rubber boots, in which she stumped away
through the water and the mud, leaving in the
latter colossal tracks which speedily became as
pond-holes in the shallower bed of the stream.
The younger woman stood at the door, gathering her dress about **her** ankles and gazing irreso-
lutely at these frightful *vestigia*, which gauged
all too accurately the depth of the mud and the
surface-water above it.

"These look like the fossil bird-tracks in the
Connecticut Valley sandstone," said Putnam,
following the direction of her eyes.

These were very large and black. She turned
them slowly on the speaker, a tallish young
fellow with a face expressive chiefly of a good-
natured audacity and an alertness for whatever
in the way of amusement might come within
range. Her look rested on him indifferently,
and then turned back to the wet gravel.

Putnam studied for a moment the back of her head and her figure, which was girlishly slender and clad in gray. "How extraordinary," he resumed, "that she should happen to have rubber boots on!"

"She keeps them in the tool-chest. The cemetery man gives her a key," she replied after a pause, and as if reluctantly. Her voice was very low and she had the air of talking to herself.

"Isn't that a rather queer place for a wardrobe? I wonder if she keeps anything else there besides the boots and the trowel and the 'sprinkle-pot'?"

"I believe she has an umbrella and some flower seeds."

"Now, if she only had a Swedish cooking-box and a patent camp-lounge," said Putnam laughing, "she could keep house here in regular style."

"She spends a great deal of time here: her children are all here, she told me."

"Well, it's an odd taste to live in a burying-ground, but one might do worse perhaps. There's nothing like getting accustomed gradually to what you've got to come to. And then if one must select a cemetery for a residence, this isn't a bad choice. Have you noticed what quaint old ways they have about it? At sunset the sexton rings a big bell that hangs in the arch over the gateway: he told me he had done it every day for twenty years. It's not done, I believe, on the principle of firing a sunset gun,

but to let people walking in the grounds know
the gate is to be shut. There's a high stone
wall, you know, and somebody might get shut
in all night. Think of having to spend the
night **here !**"

" **I have** spent the night here often," she answered, again in an absent voice and as if mur-
muring to herself.

" *You* **have?**" exclaimed Putnam. "Oh,
you slept in the tool-chest, I suppose, on the
old lady's shake-down."

She was silent, and he began to have a weird
suspicion that she had spoken in earnest. " This
is getting interesting," he said to himself; and
then aloud, " You must have seen queer sights.
Of course, when the clock struck twelve, all the
ghosts popped **out** and sat on their respective
tombstones. The ghosts in this cemetery must
be awfully old fellows. It doesn't look as if
they had buried anyone here for a hundred and
thirty-five years. I've often thought it would
be a good idea to inscribe *Complet* over the
gate, as they do on **a** Paris omnibus."

"You speak very lightly of the dead," said
the young girl in a **tone** of displeasure and
looking directly at him.

Putnam felt badly snubbed. He was about
to attempt an explanation, but her manner
indicated that she considered the conversation
at an end. She gathered up her skirts and
prepared **to** leave the summer-house. The
water had soaked away somewhat into the
gravel.

"Excuse me," said Putnam, advancing desperately and touching his hat, "but I notice that your shoes are thin and the ground is still very wet. I'm going right over to High Street, and if I can send you a carriage or anything——"

"Thank you, no: I shan't need it;" and she stepped off hastily down the walk.

Putnam looked after her till a winding of the path took her out of sight, and then started slowly homeward. "What the deuce could she mean," he pondered as he walked along, "about spending the night in the cemetery? Can she —no she can't be the gatekeeper's daughter and live in the gate-house?"

His mother and his maiden aunt, who with himself made up the entire household, received him with small scoldings and twitterings of anxiety. They felt his wet clothes, prophesied a return of his fever, and forced him to go immediately to bed, where they administered hot drinks and toast soaked in scalded milk. He lay awake a long time, somewhat fatigued and excited. In his feeble condition and in the monotony which his life had assumed of late, the trifling experience of the afternoon took on the full proportions of an adventure. He thought it over again and again, but finally fell asleep and slept soundly. He awoke once, just at dawn, and lay looking through his window at a rosy cloud which reposed upon an infinite depth of sky, motionless as if sculptured, against the blue. A light morning wind stirred the curtains and the scent of mignonette floated in from the dewy garden. He had that confused sense of anticipation **so** common in moments between waking and sleeping, when some new, pleasant thing has happened, or is to happen on the morrow, which the memory **is** too drowsy **to** present distinctly. Of this pleasant, indistinct promise that auroral cloud seemed somehow the omen or symbol, and watching it he fell asleep again. When he next awoke, the sunlight of mid-forenoon was flooding the chamber, and he **heard** his mother's voice below stairs as she sang **at her** sewing.

In the afternoon **he** started on his customary walk, and his feet **led** him involuntarily to the cemetery. As he traversed the path along the edge of the hill, he saw in one of the grave lots the heroine of his yesterday's encounter, and a sudden light broke in upon him: she was a mourner. And yet how happened it that she wore no black? There was a wooden railing round **the** enclosure, **and** within it a single mound **and a** tombstone of fresh marble. **A** few cut flowers lay on the grave. She was sitting in a low wicker chair, her hands folded in her lap, and her eyes fixed vacantly on the western hills. Putnam now took closer note of her face. It was of a brown paleness. The air of hauteur, given it by the purity of the profile and the almost insolent stare of the large black eyes, was contradicted by the sweet, irresolute curves of the mouth. At present her look expressed only a profound apathy. As he approached, her eyes turned toward him, but seemingly without recognition. Diffidence was not among Tom Putnam's failings. He felt drawn by an unconquerable sympathy and attraction to speak to her, even at the risk of intruding upon the sacredness of her grief.

"Excuse me, miss," he began, stopping in front of her, "but I want to apologize for what I said yesterday about—about the cemetery. It must have seemed very heartless to you ; but I didn't know that you were in mourning when I spoke as I did."

"I have forgotten what you said," she answered.

"I am glad you have," said Putnam rather fatuously. There seemed really nothing further to say, but as he lingered for a moment before turning away, a perverse recollection surprised him, and he laughed out loud.

She cast a look of strong indignation at him, and rose to her feet.

"Oh, I ask your pardon a thousand times," he exclaimed reddening violently. "Please don't think that I was laughing at anything to do with you. The fact is, that last idiotic speech of mine reminded me of something that happened day before yesterday. I've been sick, and I met a friend on the street who said, ' I'm glad you're better '; and I answered, ' I'm glad that you're glad that I'm better '; and then he said, ' I'm glad that you're glad that I'm glad that you're better '—like the House that Jack Built, you know—and it came over me all of a

sudden that the only way to continue our conversation gracefully would be for you to say,
'I'm glad that you're glad that I've forgotten
what you said yesterday.'"

She had listened impatiently to this naïve and
somewhat incoherent explanation, and she now
said, "I wish you would go away. You see
that I am alone here and in trouble. I can't
imagine what motive you can have for annoying
me in this way," her eyes filling with angry tears.

Putnam was too much pained by the vehe-
mence of her language to attempt any immediate
reply. His first impulse was to bow and retire
without more words. But a pertinacity which
formed one of his strongest though perhaps
least amiable traits countermanded his impulse,
and he said gravely, "Certainly, I will go at
once, but in justice to myself I must first assure
you that I didn't mean to intrude upon you or
annoy you in any way."

She sank down into her chair and averted
her face.

"You say," he continued, "that you are in
trouble, and I beg you to believe that I respect
your affliction, and that when I spoke to you
just now it was simply to ask pardon for having
hurt your feelings yesterday, without meaning
to, by my light mention of the dead. I've been
too near death's door myself lately to joke about
it." He paused, but she remained silent. "I'm
going away now," he said softly. "Won't you
say that you excuse me, and that you haven't
any hard feelings toward me?"

"Yes, oh, **yes**," she answered wearily; "I have no feelings. Please go away."

Putnam raised his hat respectfully, and went off down the pathway. On reaching the little gate-house, he **sat** down **to** rest on a bench before the door. The gatekeeper was standing **on** the threshold in his shirt-sleeves, smoking a pipe. "**A** nice day after the rain, sir," he began.

"Yes, **it** is."

"Have you any folks here, sir?"

"**No; no** one. **But** I come here sometimes for a **stroll.**"

"**Yes, I've seen** you about. Well, it's **a** nice, quiet place **for a** walk, but the grounds aint kep' up quite the shape they used to be; there aint so much occasion for it. Seems as though the buryin' business was dull, like pretty much everything else nowadays."

"Yes, that's so," replied Putnam absently.

The gatekeeper spat reflectively upon the center of the doorstep, and resumed: "There's some that comes here quite reg'lar, but they mostly have folks **here.** There's old Mrs. Lyon comes very steady, and there's young Miss Pinckney. She's one of the most reg'lar."

"Is that the young lady in gray, with black eyes?"

"That's her."

"Who is she in mourning for?"

"Well, she aint exactly in mourning. I guess, from what they say, she **aint got** the money for black bunnets and dresses, poor **gal!** But it's her brother that's buried here—last April. **He** was in the hospital learning the doctor's business when **he** was took down."

"In the hospital ? Was he from the South, do you know ? "

"Well, that **I** can't say : like enough he was."

" **Did** you say that she is poor ? "

" **So they** was telling me at the funeral. It was **a** mighty poor funeral too—not more'n **a couple of** hacks. But you can't tell much **from that, with** the fashions nowadays. Some of the richest folks buries private-like. You don't see no such funerals now as they had ten years back. **I've** seen fifty kerridges to onst a-comin' in that gate," waving his pipe impressively toward that piece of architecture, "and that was when kerridge-hire was half again as high as **it** is now. She must have spent a good sum in greenhouse flowers, though : fresh bouquets most every day she keeps a-fetchin'."

" Well, good-day," said Putnam, starting off.

" Good-day, sir."

Putnam had himself just completed his studies at the medical college when attacked by fever, and he now recalled somewhat vaguely a student of the name of Pinckney, and remembered to have heard that he was a Southerner. The gatekeeper's story increased the interest which he was beginning to feel in his new acquaintance, and he resolved to follow up his inauspicious beginnings to a better issue.

He knew that great delicacy would be **needed** in making further approaches, **and so decided to** keep out of her sight for **a time.** In the course of the next few days he ascertained, by visits to the cemetery and talks with the keeper, that she now seldom visited **her** brother's grave in the forenoon, although during the first month after his death she had **spent** all **her** days and some of her nights beside **it.**

"I hadn't the heart, sir, **to** turn **her** out **at** sundown, accordin' **to** the regulations; **so I'd** leave the gate kinder half on the jar, and she'd slip out when she had a mind to."

Putnam read the inscription on the **tomb-**stone, which **ran as follows:**

> To the Memory **of**
> HENRY PINCKNEY,
> Born October 29th, 1852.
> Died April 27th, 187–;

and under this the text:

If thou have borne him hence, tell me where thou hast laid him.

He noticed with a sudden twinge of pity that the flowers **on the** grave, though freshly picked every day, were wild flowers—mostly the common field varieties, with now **and then a** rarer **blossom from wood** or swamp, and now and then **a** garden flower. He gathered from this that the sister's purse was running low, and that she spent her mornings **in** collecting flowers outside **the city.** His imagination dwelt tenderly upon her slim, young figure and mourning face passing through far-away fields and along the margins of lonely creeks in search of some new bloom which grudging Nature might yield her for her sorrowful needs. Meanwhile he determined that the shrine of her devotion **should** not want richer offerings. There **was** a hothouse on the way from his home to the cemetery, **and** he now stopped **there** occasionally of a morning and bought a few roses to lay upon the mound. This continued for **a** fortnight, He noticed that his offerings were left to wither undisturbed, though the little bunches of field flowers were daily renewed as before.

In spite of the funereal nature of his occupation, his spirits in these days were extraordinarily high. His life, so lately escaped from the shadows of death, seemed to enjoy a rejuvenescence and to put forth fresh blossoms in the summer air. As he sat under the cedars and listened to the buzzing of the flies that frequented the shade, the unending sound grew **to** be an assurance of earthly immortality. His new lease of existence prolonged itself into a **fee** simple, and even in presence of the monuments of decay his future, filled with bright hazy dreams, melted softly into eternity. But one morning, as he approached the little grave-lot with his accustomed offerings, he looked up and saw the young girl standing before him. Her eyes were fixed on the flowers in his hand. He colored guiltily and stood still, like a boy caught robbing **an** orchard. She **looked both surprised and** embarrassed, but said at once, **"If you are the** gentleman who has been **put-**ting flowers on my brother's grave, I thank you for his sake——"

She paused, and **he** broke in : " I ought to explain, Miss Pinckney, that I have a better right than you think, perhaps, to bring these flowers here. I was a fellow-student with your brother in the medical school."

Her expression changed immediately. " Oh, did you know my brother ? " she asked eagerly.

He felt like a wretched hypocrite as he answered, **" Yes, I** knew him, though not intimately exactly. But I took—I take—a very strong interest in him."

"Everyone loved Henry who knew him," she said, " **but** his class have all been graduated and gone away, and he made few friends, because he was **so shy.** No one comes near him now but me."

He was silent. She walked to the grave and he followed, and they stood there without speaking. It did not seem to occur to her to ask why he had not mentioned her brother at their former interview. She was evidently of an unsuspecting nature, or else all other impressions were forgotten and absorbed in the **one** thought of her bereavement. After **a** glance at her, Putnam ventured to lay his roses reverently upon the mound. She held in her hand a few wild flowers just gathered. These she kissed, and dropped **them** also on the grave.

He understood the meaning of her gesture and was deeply moved.

" Poor, little, dull-colored things," she said, looking down at them.

" They **are** a thousand times more beautiful than mine," he exclaimed passionately ; " I am ashamed **of** those heartless affairs : anybody can buy them."

"Oh, no. **My brother** was very fond of roses. Perhaps you remember his taste for them ?" she inquired innocently.

" I—I don't think **he** ever alluded to them. The atmosphere of the medical college was not very æsthetic, **you** know."

" At first **I** used **to** bring greenhouse flowers," she continued, without much heeding his answer, **"**but lately I haven't been able to afford them except on Sundays. Sundays I bring **white ones** from the greenhouse."

She had seated herself in her wicker chair, and Putnam, after a moment's hesitation, sat down on the low railing near her. He observed, among the wild plants that she had gathered, the mottled leaves and waxy blossoms of the pipsissewa and its cousin the shinleaf.

" You have been a long way to get some of those," he said. " That pipsissewa grows in hemlock woods, and the nearest are several miles from here."

" I don't know their names. I found them in a wood where I used to walk sometimes with my brother. *He* knew all their names. I went there **very** early **this** morning, **when the dew** was on them."

"' **Flowers that have on them the cold** dews of the night are strewings fittest for graves,'" said Putnam in an undertone.

Her face had assumed its usual absent ex-**pression,** and she seemed busy with some memory, and unconscious of **his** presence. He recalled the latter to her by rising and saying, " I will bid **you** good-morning now, but **I** hope you will let me come and sit here sometimes if **it doesn't** disturb you. I have **been** very sick myself lately : I was near dying of the typhoid **fever.** I think it does me good to come here."

"**Did** you have the typhoid **?** My brother died of the typhoid."

" May I come sometimes **? "**

" You may come if you wish to visit Henry. But please don't bring any more of those ex-pensive flowers. **I** suppose it is selfish in me, but I can't bear to have any of his friends do more for him than I can."

" I won't bring any more, of course, if it troubles you, and I thank you very much for letting me come. Good-morning, Miss Pinck-ney." He bowed and walked away.

Putnam availed himself discreetly of the per-mission given. He came occasionally of **an** afternoon, and **sat** for an hour at **a time.** Usually she **said** little. Her silence appeared **to** proceed not from reserve, **but** from dejec-tion. Sometimes she spoke **of her** brother. Putnam learned that he had been her only near relative. Their parents had died in **her** childhood, and she had come **North** with **her** brother when he entered the medical school. **From** something that she once said, Putnam **inferred that** her brother had owned an annuity which died with him, and that she had been left with little **or** nothing. They had few acquaint-**ances in** the North, almost none in the city. **An** aunt in the South had offered her a home, **and she** was going there in the fall. **She** looked forward with dread to the time of **her** departure.

"It will be so cruel," she said, "to leave my poor boy all alone here among strangers, and I never away from him before."

"Don't think of it now," he answered, "and when you are gone **I** will come here often and see to everything."

Her bereavement had evidently benumbed all her faculties and left her with **a** slight hold on life. She had no hopes or wishes for the future. In alluding to **her** brother she confused her tenses, speaking of him sometimes in the past, and sometimes **in** the present as of one still alive. Putnam felt that in a girl of her age this mood was too unnatural to last, and he reckoned not unreasonably on the reaction that must come when her youth began again to assert its rights. He was now thoroughly in love, and as he sat watching her beautiful, abstracted face, he found it hard to keep back some expression of tenderness. Often, too, it was difficult for him to tone down his spirits to the proper pitch of respectful sympathy with her grief. His existence was golden with new-found life and hope; into the shadow that covered hers he could not enter. He could only endeavor to draw her out into the sunshine once more.

One day the two were sitting, as usual, in silence or speaking but rarely. It was a day in the very core of summer, and the life of Nature was at its flood. The shadows of the trees rested so heavy and motionless on the grass that they appeared to sink into it and weigh it down like palpable substances.

" I feel," said Putnam suddenly, "as though I should live forever."

" Did you ever doubt it ? " she asked.

"Oh, I mean here — in the body. I can't conceive of death or of a spiritual existence on such a day as this."

" There is nothing here to live for," she said wearily. Presently she added, " This hot glare makes me sick. I wish those men would stop hammering on the bridge. I wish I could die and get away into the dark."

Putnam paused before replying. He had never heard her speak so impatiently. Was the revulsion coming ? Was she growing tired of sorrow ? After a minute he said, " Ah, you don't know what it is to be a convalescent and lie for months in a darkened room listening to the hand-organ man and the scissors-grinder, and the fellow that goes through the streets hallooing ' Cash paid for rags ! ' It's like having a new body to get the use of your limbs again and come out into the sunshine."

"Were you very sick?" she inquired with some show of interest.

He remembered with some mortification that he had told **her** so once or twice before. She had apparently forgotten it. "Yes, I nearly died."

"Were you glad to recover?"

"Well, I can't remember that I had any feelings in particular when I first struck the up-track. It was hard work fighting for life, and I don't **think** I cared much **one** way or the other. But when I got well **enough** to sit up it began to grow interesting. I used to sit at the window in a very infantile frame of mind and watch everything that went by. It wasn't a very rowdy life, as the prisoner in solitary confinement said to Dickens. We live in a back street, where there's not much passing. The advent of the baker's cart used to be the chief excitement. It was painted red and yellow, and he baked very nice leaf-cookies. My mother would hang a napkin in the door-knocker when she wanted him to stop; and as I couldn't see the knocker from my window, I used to make bets with Dummy as to whether the wagon would stop or not."

"Your mother is living, then?"

"Yes; my father died when I was a boy."

She asked no further questions, but a few minutes after rose and said, "I think I will go now. Good-evening."

He had never before outstayed her. He looked at his watch and found that it was only half-past four.

"I hope," he began anxiously, "that you are not feeling sick: you spoke just now of being oppressed by the heat. Excuse me for staying so long."

"Oh, no," she answered, "I'm not sick. I reckon I need a little rest. Good-evening."

Putnam lingered after she was gone. He found his way to his old bench under the cedars and sat there for a while. He had not occupied this seat since his first meeting with Miss Pinckney in the summer-house, and the initials which he had whittled on its edge impressed him as belonging to some bygone stage of his history. This was the first time that she had questioned him about himself. His sympathy had won her confidence, but she had treated him hitherto in an impersonal way, as something tributary to her brother's memory, like his tombstone or the flowers on his grave. The suspicion that he was seeking her for her own sake had not, so far as Putnam could discover, ever entered her thoughts.

But in the course of their next few interviews there came a change in her behavior. The simplicity and unconsciousness of her sorrow had become complicated with some other feeling. He caught her looking at him narrowly once or twice, and when he looked hard at her there was visible in her manner a soft agitation—something which in a girl of more sanguine complexion might have been interpreted as a blush. She sometimes suffered herself to be coaxed a little way into talking of things remote from the subject of her sorrow. Occasionally she questioned Putnam shyly about himself, and he needed but slight encouragement to wax confidential. She listened quietly to his experiences, and even smiled now and then at something that he said. His heart beat high with triumph: he fancied that he was leading her slowly up out of the Valley of the Shadow of Death.

But the upward path was a steep one. She had many sudden relapses and changes of **mood.** Putnam divined that she felt her grief loosening its tight hold on her and slipping away, and that she clung to it as a consecrated thing with a morbid fear of losing it altogether. There were days when her demeanor betokened a passionate self-reproach, as though she accused herself secretly of wronging her brother and profaning his tomb in allowing more cheer-**ful** thoughts to blunt the edge of her bereave-**ment.** He remarked also that her eyes were **often** red from weeping. There sometimes mingled with her remorse a plain resentment toward himself. At such times she would hardly speak to him, and the slightest gayety or even cheerfulness on his part was received as downright heartlessness. He made a practice, therefore, of withdrawing at once whenever he found her in this frame of mind.

One day they had been sitting long together.

She had appeared unusually content, but had
spoken little. The struggle in her heart had
perhaps worn itself out for the present, and she
had yielded to the warm current of life and
hope which was bearing her back into the sunshine. Suddenly the elderly woman who had
formed one of the company in the summer-
house, on the day of the thunder storm, passed
along the walk with her trowel and watering-
pot. She nodded to Miss Pinckney, and then
pausing opposite the pair, glanced sharply from
one to the other, smiled significantly and passed
on. This trifling incident aroused Putnam's
companion from her reverie: she looked at
him with a troubled expression and said,
"Do you think you ought to come here so
much?"

"Why not?"

"I don't know. How well did you know my
brother Henry?"

"If I didn't know him so very intimately when
he was living, I feel that I know him well now
from all that you have told me about him.
And, if you will pardon my saying so, I feel
that I know his sister a little too, and have
some title to her acquaintance."

"You have been very kind, and I am grate-
ful for it, but perhaps you ought not to come so
much."

"I'm sorry if I have come too much," rejoined
Putnam bitterly, "but I shall not come much
more. I am going away soon. The doctor
says I am not getting along fast enough and

must have change of air. He has ordered **me** to the mountains."

There was silence for **a** few minutes. He was looking moodily down at the turf, pulling a blade of grass now and then, biting it, and throwing it away.

"I thank you very much for your sympathy and kindness," she said at length, rising from her chair; "and I hope you will recover very fast **in** the mountains. Good-by."

She extended her hand, which Putnam took and held. It was trembling perceptibly. "Wait a moment," he said. "Before I go I should like to show some little mark of respect to your brother's memory. Won't you meet me at the greenhouse to-morrow morning—say about nine o'clock—and select **a** few flowers? They will be your flowers, you know—your of-fering."

"Yes," she answered, "**I** will; and I thank you again for him."

The next morning at the appointed hour Putnam descended the steps into the green-house. The gardener had just watered the plants. A rich steam exhaled from the earth and clouded all the glass, and the moist air was heavy with the breath of heliotropes and roses. A number of butterflies were flying about, and at the end of a many-colored perspective of leaves and blossoms, Putnam saw Miss Pinckney hovering around a collection of tropical orchids. The gardener had passed on into an adjoining hothouse, and no sound broke the quiet but the dripping of **water in** a tank of aquatic **plants.** The fans of **the** palms **and** the **long fronds of the** tree-ferns hung as still **as in some painting** of an Indian **isle.**

She greeted him with a smile and held out her hand to him. The beauty of the morning and of the place had wrought in her a gentle intoxication, and the mournful nature of her errand was for the moment forgotten. "Isn't it delicious here?" she exclaimed; "I think I should like to live in a greenhouse and grow like a plant."

" A little of that kind of thing would do you no end of good," he replied; "a little concentrated sunshine and bright colors and the smell of the fresh earth, you know. If you **were** my patient, I would make you take a course **of it.** I'd say you wanted more vegetable tissue, **and** prescribe a greenhouse for six months. **I've no** doubt this man here would take you. **A** young lady apprentice would be quite an attractive feature. You could pull off dead leaves and strike graceful attitudes, training up vines, like the gardener's daughter in Tennyson."

" What are those gorgeous things?" she asked, pointing **to a row** of orchids hung on nails along the wall.

" Those are epiphytic orchids—air plants, you know: they require no earth for their roots: they live on the air."

" Like a chameleon?"

" Like a chameleon."

He took down from its nail one of the little

wooden slabs, and showed her the roots coiled about it, with the cluster of bulbs. The flower was snow-white and shaped like a butterfly. The fringe of the lip was of a delicate rose-pink, and at the base of it were two spots of rich maroon, each with a central spot of the most **vivid** orange. Every color was as pronounced as though it were the only one.

"What a daring combination!" she cried. "If a lady should dress in all those colors she'd be thought vulgar, but somehow it doesn't seem vulgar in a flower."

She turned the blossom over and looked at the under side of the petals. "Those orange spots show right through the leaf," she went on. "as if they were painted and the paint laid on thick."

"Do you know," said Putnam, "that what you've just said gives me a good deal of encouragement?"

"Encouragement? How?"

"Well, it's the first really feminine thing—— At least—no, I don't mean that. But it makes **me** think that you are more like other girls."

His explanation was interrupted by the entrance of the gardener.

"Will you select some of those orchids, please —if you like them, that is?" asked Putnam.

A shade passed over her face. "They are too gay for his—for Henry," she answered.

"Try to tolerate a little brightness to-day," he pleaded in a low voice. "You must dedicate this morning to me; it's the last, you know."

" I will take a few of them if you wish it, but not this one. I will take that little white one and that large purple one."

The gardener reached down the varieties which she pointed out, and they passed along the alley to select other flowers. She chose a number of white roses, dark-shaded fuchsias and English violets, and then they left the place. Her expression had grown thoughtful, though not precisely sad. They walked slowly up the long shady street leading to the cemetery.

"I am dropping some of the flowers," she said, stopping; "will you carry these double fuchsias a minute, please, while I fasten the others?"

He took them and laughed. " Now, if this were in a novel," he said, "what a neat opportunity for me to say, 'May I not *always* carry your double fuchsias?'"

She looked at him quickly, and her brown cheek blushed rosy red, but she started on without making any reply and walked faster.

"She takes," he said to himself. But he saw the cemetery gate at the end of the street. " I must make this walk last longer," he thought. Accordingly he invented several cunning devices to prolong it, stopping now and then to point out something worth noting in the handsome grounds which lined the street. And so they sauntered along, she appearing to have forgotten the speech which embarrassed her, or at least she did not resent it. They paused in front of a well-kept lawn, and he drew her attention to the turf. "**It**'s almost as dark as the evergreens," he said.

"Yes," she answered, "**it's so** green that it's almost blue."

"What do you suppose makes the bees gather round that croquet stake so?"

"I reckon they take the bright colors on it for flowers," she answered, with a certain quaintness of fancy which he had often remarked in her.

As they stood there, leaning against the fence, **a** party of schoolgirls came along with their satchels and spelling-books. They giggled and stared as they passed the fence, and one of them, **a** handsome, long-legged, bold-faced thing, said aloud, "Oh, my! look at me and my fancy beau a-takin' a walk!"

Putnam glanced at his companion, who colored nervously and looked away. "Saucy little giglets!" he laughed. "Did you hear what she said?"

"**Yes**," almost inaudibly.

"**I** hope it didn't annoy you?"

"It was very rude," walking on.

"Well, I rather like naughty schoolgirls: they are amusing creatures. When I was a very small boy I was sent to a girl's school, and I used to study their ways. They always had crumbs in their apron pockets; they used to write on a slate, 'Tommy is a good boy,' and hold it up for me to see when the teacher wasn't looking; they borrowed my geography at recess and painted all the pictures vermilion and yellow." He paused, but she said nothing, and he continued, talking against time. "There was one piece of chewing-gum in that school which circulated from mouth to mouth. It had been originally spruce gum, I believe, but it was masticated beyond recognition : the parent tree wouldn't have known her child. One day I found it hidden away on a window-sill behind the shutter. It was flesh-colored and dented all over with the marks of sharp little teeth. I kept that chewing-gum for a week, and the school was like a cow that's lost her cud."

As Putnam completed these reminiscences they entered the cemetery gate, and the shadow of its arch seemed to fall across the young girl's soul. The bashful color had faded from her cheek and the animation from her eye. Her face wore a troubled expression ; she walked slowly and looked about at the grave-stones.

Putnam stopped talking abruptly, but presently said, "You have not asked me for your fuchsias."

She stood still and held out her hand for them.

"I thought you might be meaning to let me keep them," said Putnam. His heart beat fast and his voice trembled as he continued : "Perhaps you thought that what I said a while ago was said in joke, but I mean it in real earnest."

"Mean what ? " she asked faintly.

"Don't you know what I mean?" he said, coming near and taking her hand. "Shall I tell you, darling?"

"Oh, please don't! Oh, I think I know. Not here—not now. Give me the flowers," she said, disengaging her hand, "and I will put them on Henry's grave."

He handed them to her and said, **"** I won't go on now if it troubles you; but tell me first— I am going away to-morrow, and shan't be back till October—shall I find you **here** then, and **may** I speak then?"

" I shall be here till winter."

" And may I speak then?"

" Yes."

" And will you listen?"

" Yes."

"Then I can wait."

They moved on again along **the** cemetery walks. Putnam felt an exultation that he could not suppress. In spite of her language, her face and the tone of her voice had betrayed her. He knew that she cared for him. But in the blindness of his joy he failed to notice an increasing agitation in her manner, which foretold **the** approach of some painful crisis of feeling. Her conflicting emotions, long pent up, were now in most delicate equilibrium. The slightest shock might throw them out of balance. Putnam's nature, though generous and at bottom sympathetic, lacked the fineness of insight needed to interpret the situation. Like many **men** of robust and heedless temperament,

he was more used **to bend others' moods** to his
own than to enter fully into their's. His way of
approaching the subject had been unfortunate,
beginning as **he had with** a jest. The sequel
was destined **to be** still more unlucky.

They had reached a part of the cemetery
which was not divided **into lots, but** formed a
sort of burial commons for the **behoof** of the
poor. It was used mainly by Germans, **and** the
graves were principally those of children. **The**
headstones were wooden, **painted** white, **with in-**
scriptions **in** black or gilt lettering. Humble
edgings of white pebbles or shells, partly em-
bedded **in** the earth, bordered some of the
graves ; artificial flowers, tinsel crosses, hearts
and other such fantastic decorations lay upon
the mounds. Putnam's companion paused with
an expression **of** pity before one of these **un-**
couth sepulchers, **a** little heap **of** turf which
covered the body of a " span-long babe."

" Now, isn't that *echt Deutsch?* " began Putnam, whom the gods had made mad. " Is that
glass affair let into the tombstone a looking-
glass or **a portrait** of the deceased—like that
' **statoot of a deceased** infant ' that Holmes
tells about ? Even our ancestral cherub and
willow **tree** are better than that, **or** even the inevitable sick lamb and broken lily."

" The **people are** poor," **she** murmured.

" They **do** the same **sort of** thing when
they're rich. It's the national taste to stick little tawdry fribbles all over the face of Nature."

" Poor little baby ! " she said gently.

"It's a rather old baby by this time," rejoined Putnam, pointing out the date on the wooden slab—"Eighteen fifty-one: it would be older than I now, if it had kept on."

Her eyes fell upon the inscription, and she read it aloud: "Hier ruht in Gott, Heinrich Franz, Geb. Mai 13, 1851. Gest. August 4, 1852. Wir hoffen auf Wiedersehen." She repeated the last words softly to herself.

"Are those white things cobblestones, or what?" continued Putnam perversely, indicating the border which quaintly encircled the little mound. "As I live," he exclaimed, "they are door-knobs!" and partly through carelessness, partly through accident, he poked one of them out of the ground with the end of his cane.

"Stop!" she cried vehemently; "how can you do that?"

He dropped his cane and looked at her in wonder. She burst into tears and turned away. "You think I am a heartless brute?" he cried remorsefully, hastening after her.

"Oh, go away, please—go away and leave me alone. I am going to my brother; I want to be alone."

She hurried on, and he paused irresolute. "Miss Pinckney!" he called after her, but she made no response. His instinct, now aroused too late, told him that he had better leave her alone for the present. So he picked up his walking stick and turned reluctantly homeward. He cursed himself mentally as he retraced the paths along which they had walked together a few moments before. " I'm a fool," he said to himself ; " I've gone and upset it all. Couldn't I see that she was feeling badly? I suppose I imagined that I was funny, and she thought I was an insensible brute. This comes of giving way to my infernal high spirits." At the same time a shade of resentment mingled with his self-reproaches. " Why can't she be a little more cheerful and like other girls, and make some allowance for a fellow?" he asked. " Her brother wasn't everybody else's brother. It's downright morbid, this obstinate woe of hers. Other people have lost friends and got over it."

On the morrow he was to start for the mountains. He visited the cemetery in the morning. but Miss Pinckney was not there. He did not know her address, nor could the gatekeeper inform him ; and in the afternoon he set out on his journey with many misgivings.

It was early October when Putnam returned to the city. He went at once to the cemetery, but on reaching the grave his heart sank at the sight of a bunch of withered flowers which must have lain many days upon the mound. The blossoms were black and the stalks brittle and dry. " Can she have changed her mind and gone South already?" he asked himself.

There was a new sexton in the gate-house, who could tell him nothing about her. He wandered through the grounds, looking for the old woman with the watering-pot, but the season had grown cold, and she had probably

ceased her gardening operations for the year.
He continued his walk beyond the marshes.
The woods had grown rusty and the sandy pastures outside the city were ringing with the incessant creak of grasshoppers, which rose in
clouds under his feet as he brushed though the
thin grass. The blue-curl and the life-everlast-
ing distilled their pungent aroma in the autumn
sunshine. A feeling of change and forlornness
weighed upon his spirit. As with Thomas of
Ercildoune, whom the Queen of Faëry carried
away into Eildon Hill, the short period of his
absence seemed seven years long. An old English song came into his head:

> Winter wakeneth all my care,
> Now these leavës waxeth bear:
> Oft it cometh in my thought,
> Of this worldës joy how it goeth all to naught.

Soon after arriving at the hills he had written
to Miss Pinckney a long letter of explanations
and avowals; but he did not know the number
of her lodgings, nor, oddly enough, even her
Christian name, and the letter had been returned
to him unopened. The next month was one of
the unhappiest in Putnam's life. On returning
to the city, thoroughly restored in health, he
had opened an office, but he found it impossible
to devote himself quietly to the duties of his
profession. He visited the cemetery at all hours,
but without success. He took to wandering
about in remote quarters and back streets of
the town, and eyed sharply every female figure

that passed him in the twilight, especially if it walked quickly or wore a veil. He slept little at night, and grew restless and irritable. He had never confided this experience even to his mother; it seemed to him something apart.

One afternoon, toward the middle of November, he was returning homeward weary and dejected from a walk in the suburbs. His way led across an uninclosed outskirt of the town which served as a common to the poor people of the neighborhood. It was traversed by a score of footpaths, and frequented by goats, and by ducks that dabbled in the puddles of rain water collected in the hollows. Halfway across this open tract stood what had formerly been an old-fashioned country house, now converted into a soap-boiling establishment. Around this was a clump of old pine trees, the remnant of a grove which had once flourished in the sandy soil. There was something in the desolation of the place that flattered Putnam's mood, and he stopped to take it in. The air was dusk, but embers of an angry sunset burned low in the west. A cold wind made a sound in the pine tops like the beating of surf on a distant shore. A flock of little winter birds flew suddenly up from the ground into one of the trees, like a flight of gray leaves whirled up by a gust. As Putnam turned to look at them he saw, against the strip of sunset along the horizon, the slim figure of a girl walking rapidly toward the opposite side of the common. His heart gave a great leap, and he started after her

on a run.   At a corner of the open ground the
figure vanished, nor could Putnam decide into
which of two or three small streets she had
turned.   He ran down one and up another, but
met no one except a few laborers coming home
from work, and finally gave up the quest.   But
this momentary glimpse produced in him a new
excitement.   He felt sure that he had not been
mistaken ; he knew the swift, graceful step, the
slight form bending in the wind.   He fancied
that he had even recognized the poise and shape
of the little head.   He imagined, too, that he
had not been unobserved, and that she had
some reason for avoiding him.   For a week or
more he haunted the vicinity of the common,
but without result.   December was already
drawing to an end when he received the following note :

DEAR MR. PUTNAM :
   You must forgive me for running away from you
the other evening.   I am right—am I not—in sup-
posing that you saw and recognized me ?   It was
rude in me not to wait for you, but I had not courage
to talk with anyone just then.   Perhaps I should
have seen you before at the cemetery—if you still
walk there—but I have been sick and have not been
there for a long time.   I was only out for the first
time when I saw you last Friday.   My aunt has sent
for me, and I am going South in a few days.   I shall
leave directions to have this posted to you as soon as
I am gone.
   I promised to be here when you came back, and
I write this to thank you for your kind interest in me

and to explain why I go away without seeing **you** again. I think that I know what you wanted **to** ask **me** that **day that we** went to the greenhouse, and perhaps under happier circumstances I could **have** given you the answer which you wished. But I **have** seen so much **sorrow, and** I am of such a gloomy disposition that **I am not fit for** cheerful society, and I know you would regret **your** choice.

I shall think very often and **very** gratefully of you, and shall not forget the words **on** that little German baby's gravestone. Good-by.

IMOGEN PINCKNEY.

Putnam felt stunned and benumbed on first reading **this letter.** Then he read **it** over mechanically **two or** three times. The date was a month old, but the postmark showed that it had just been mailed. She must have postponed her departure somewhat after writing it, or the person with whom **it** had been left had neglected to post **it** till now. He felt a sudden oppression and **need of** air, and taking his hat left the house. It was evening, and the first snow of the season lay deep on the ground. Anger and grief divided his heart. " It's too bad ! too bad !" he murmured, with tears in his eyes ; " she might have given me one chance to speak. She hasn't been fair to me. What's the matter with her, **anyhow ?** She has brooded and brooded till she is downright melancholy-mad ;" and then with a revulsion of feeling : " My poor darling girl ! **Here** she has been, sick and all alone, sitting day after day in that cursed graveyard. I ought never to have gone to the moun-

tains; I ought to have stayed. I might have
known how it would turn out. Well, it's **all**
over now, I suppose."

He had taken, half unconsciously, the direction of the cemetery, and now found himself at
the entrance. The gate was locked, but he
climbed over the wall and waded through the
snow to the spot where he had sat with her so
many summer afternoons. The wicker chair
was buried out of sight in **a** drift. A scarcely
visible undulation **in** the white level marked the
position **of** the mound, and the headstone had a
snow cap. The cedars stood black in the dim
moonlight, and the icy coating of their boughs
rattled like candelabra. He stood a few moments near the railing, and then tore the letter into
fragments and threw them on the snow. "There!
good-by, good-by!" he said bitterly, as the wind
carried them skating away over the crust.

But what was that? The moon cast a
shadow of Henry Pinckney's headstone on the
snow, but what was that other and similar
shadow beyond it? Putnam had been standing
edgewise to the slab; he shifted his position
now and saw **a** second stone and a second
mound side by side with the first. An awful
faintness and trembling seized him as he approached it and bent his head close down to the
marble. The jagged shadows of the cedar
branches played across the surface, but by the
uncertain light he could read the name "Imogen
Pinckney," and below **it** the inscription, "Wir
hoffen auf Wiedersehen."

VII.

EDRIC THE WILD AND THE WITCH WIFE.

EDRIC THE WILD AND THE WITCH WIFE.

THAT the unseen **powers are** female appears from the capricious way in which they bestow their favors. You shall have a spiritually minded man in **search** of the marvelous all his life, and yet never see so much as a ghost. He is abroad at the most propitious seasons; in windy autumn twilights, and in the hours of deepest sleep, toward morning, when the moon is low. He fasts to purge his sense of grossness and make his vision clear. Sometimes he wakes a whole summer night and wanders about **the** dusky fields, the edges of woods and marshes and all haunted places, yet never hears anything more evil than the boom **of** the nighthawk hunting insects **in** the heavens, or the iterations of a whip-poor-will from **a tree** in the meadow. **But** some wild boon companion, some Tam O'Shanter, who drinks deep and sleeps sound, and never troubles his head about wraiths and fairies, has but to lose his way anywhere after nightfall, when—presto! **the** curtains of the invisible world are drawn aside and his drunken eyes are staring on the mad dances of goblins, for an instant glimpse of which many a better man would give ten years of his life.

The conditions **on** which the powers grant their rare favors to men are easy but, once violated, the givers are inexorable. They are the lords of a manor held at some trifling rental—an annual shoat or hare. But the rent **must be** paid. **The** very easiness of the condition leads the recipient of their bounties to neglect **it.** " What ! " he thinks in his heart, " the gods will never exact such a toy." And then he finds too late that his right is forfeit beyond recall, **and his** lords stand upon the letter of the bond. Naaman, the Syrian, thought it a light matter to bathe in Jordan, and would have chosen some more difficult way to be healed **of** his leprosy ; and Orpheus did but glance behind him to lose his wife and find the truth :

By the just gods whom no weak pity moved.

This also found Edric the Wild, the Saxon thane, who stood out for four years against William the Conqueror. Edric " Salvage " and " Silvaticus," he is described in Domesday Book, where he is entered as lord of the manor of Ledbury North. And old Simeon of Durham calls him **a** *vir strenuissimus*, who laid waste the lands of the castellans of Hereford, and killed many of their knights and squires. He lurked, with his following of Saxon outlaws, in **the** forests and hills of the rough Welsh border, and made his peace with the Normans

only in 1070, when resistance to the foreign
rule had become hopeless. He was then taken
into the favor of William—who, like a later
monarch of England, "loved a man"—and
made the expedition to Scotland with him in
1072. So much is history; but legend, hardly
less authentic than the chronicles of those dim
times, says as follows :

Edric, returning late one night from a hunt,
lost his way in the great oak forests which
filled the valley of the Dee. He was attended
by a single horse-boy, who nodded half asleep
on his horse, as he followed his master slowly
along a narrow wood-road that wound between the thick boles of the oak trees and the
clumps of gigantic fern. The night was a
wild one, with a high wind and a scud of clouds
across the gibbous moon. There was a steady
war in the tree-tops, lower down a groaning
and shrieking in the boughs, and lower still a
whistle and rustle in the fern. All these sounds
occasionally assumed a resemblance to human
voices, and the wavering moon shadows that
ran along the path seemed every now and
then to be fantastic shapes of living creatures,
that raced ahead of the riders, to hide behind a
trunk and then dart out and race on again. It
was a haunted region, "where Deva spreads
her wizard stream," full of the memory of Merlin and not far from the waste city of Chester,
on whose walls, the few Saxon churls that
sometimes took shelter there in stormy weather
still saw the apparitions of Roman sentries

making their nightly rounds. But Edric was not superstitious. He was a rough-and-ready soldier, distinguished, says Walter Map, *corporis agilitate et jocunditate verborum et operum*. The horses stumbled on till the wood-path broadened into a glade, in the middle of which **a** deserted hunting lodge broke the moonlight with its dark bulk. Here Edric and his squire took lodging for the night, after hob-**bling** their horses and turning them loose to **crop** the grass in the little clearing. They **found the** lodge unfurnished save for a few shreds **of** worm-eaten arras that waved and flapped in the gusty air. But groping their way through hall and bower, **they** finally came upon a heap of leaves which the winds of many autumns had driven through **the** empty casements and piled up in the corner of a bare chamber. There they made their bed and were soon asleep. It was long past midnight when Edric awoke. The wind had fallen and the **moon** was down, but a light streamed through **the** door of the neighboring apartment, whence also issued an indescribable sound. The boy was still asleep and the master, grasping his short *seax* or Saxon sword, stole to the door and looked in. The room was full of light, the source of which, however, was invisible ; as also of the whirring, buzzing noise which sounded, as much as anything, like the continuous rustle of ten thousand clocks that hang upon the wall of the *Uhrausstellung* at Triberg in the Black Forest, and keep up **a** humming as of a myriad insects. Through this pierced **at intervals** the **twanging of** a Welsh harp, though **the** harper was nowhere to be seen. In the **center** of the room a **score of** women moved **to and** fro in a sort of choral dance, chanting a low song in a tongue which was neither Welsh nor English, both of which languages **were** familiar to the hardy borderer. The **dancers** were very fair, tall as men, and clad in light **tunics** of white linen. Edric gazed until his eyes grew dazzled and his head swam. He had **no** doubt as to the true **nature of** the beings that he saw before him. He **had** heard **of the** nocturnal phalanxes of demons and the vengeance which they were wont **to** wreak upon **the** venturesome mortals who violated their divinities and exposed their rites. **But** his blood was up and the daredevil spirit of the outlaw prompted him **to** go all lengths. Gradually **his** gaze became concentrated upon a single figure, the tallest **and** most beautiful witch in **the** band. **He devoured** her graceful motions with his eyes, as she wheeled and leaped, linked and unlinked herself in **the choral** chain, till the impulse to break the spell **by** action became overpowering, and, dropping his sword, he rushed into the group with **a shout** and seized the beautiful sorceress in his **arms.** Instantly the music stopped with **a** loud rattling and jarring sound, and the companions of his captive, swarming about him like angry bees, assailed him with teeth and nails. His prize, too, writhed and twisted in his **grasp,** but **he held her** fast and shouted lustily for the boy. **At** last the latter, with pale face and chattering teeth, appeared in the doorway, and immediately all was darkness and silence. So suddenly had the apparitions vanished that Edric almost thought that the creature which he held had vanished too. But, no ; in the darkness he still felt the warm flesh palpitating in his embrace, heard her thick pantings, and even smelled the sweet breath of her lips. She made no further resistance, while her captor led her out from the lodge into the open air, where the gray light of dawn shone into her wild eyes. The boy caught the horses and led them up, and Edric, seating her before him on the saddle, rode slowly off into the woods, looking warily into the thickets on either side, as fearful of an ambush. But he met with no disturbance, and soon the forest about began to have a familiar look, and before the noon was high he had brought her home to Ladbury.

For three days she uttered no word, but she yielded herself patiently to his caresses, and it is **said** that he found in her embraces a delight beyond all pleasure which a mortal woman can impart. On the fourth day she said to him in good West Saxon, "I salute you, my dearest lord. You will be safe and prosperous until you reproach me, either with my sisters or the place where you found me, or with any circumstances connected therewith. From that day you will lose me, and decline from your felicity, and die before your time, through your importunity."

So Edric made a **great** feast and **bade** the neighboring earls to it, and **was solemnly** wedded to his sylvan bride. Her fame reached the court, and King William summoned her with her husband to London for a season, Edric having now made his peace with the Conqueror and received from him the manor of Ledbury North in fief. At court her unheard of beauty was the wonder of all the nobles **and** the ladies.

She bore **her** husband a boy, Alnodus, who differed seemingly in no respect from the **fruit** of ordinary marriages. Edric lived happily with his wife for many years, but **at** last he grew careless and secure. She was of a still conversation and had some elfish ways, though not unpleasing ones. She would laugh and talk in a low tone to herself. If Edric woke in the night he always found her waking. She loved to walk through solitary pastures at dew-fall, at which times she could **be** heard at **a** great distance singing a peculiar song. Sometimes she disappeared for hours at a time, none knew whither, but this was always by day. At length, however, Edric, returning from the hunt about the third hour of the night, sought her in **her** chamber, and **not** finding her there called her. She came slowly from somewhere when called, and Edric, looking **upon her, said in** sudden anger and impatience, "Have **your sisters** been keeping you?" **The rest of** his speech, says the chronicler, was uttered to **air,** for, in the instant, at the **mention of** her sisters, she vanished **and was** never **seen** again. In vain her deserted mate sought the enchanted glade and the old hunting lodge where he had won her. He traced and retraced every path through the forest till each tree and bush had grown familiar, but never found the spot. He called her name day and night with tears, with prayers for forgiveness, with promises of amends. But naught availed, and he wasted away with grief and died in a few short months after her disappearance.

Of his son Alnodus, who survived him, it **is** related that he became a man of great sanctity and wisdom, who, being struck with palsy and **a** tremor of the head and limbs when still young, had himself carried to Hereford to the shrine of **St.** Ethelbert, king and martyr, and praying before his altar was restored in a single night to sound health. In gratitude for this miraculous interposition, he gave his manor of Ledbury to God and the Blessed Virgin and St. Ethelbert, with all its appurtenances in perpetuity, and **it** is now annexed to the episcopal see of Hereford. He himself, having stripped him of his entire possessions, spent the rest of his life **as** a pilgrim in the service of Christ.

VIII.

THE WINE-FLOWER.

THE WINE-FLOWER.

HAT is a mushroom, Thomas, a little button mushroom ; and there is another, and still another. They spring up where the turf is smooth and thick and nibbled close by the sheep. Notice their flesh-colored gills and the ruptured edges of the white membrane that covered them, as delicate as the softest undressed kid-skin. Smell their earthy fragrance. Break off this stem and take a bite of it. It tastes like a hickory-nut, without its oil. These little fungi start up in a single night, as if begotten by the dew and the starlight. But we have heard of plants that had an even quicker growth. There was Jack's beanstalk, and Jonah's gourd, and the blossoming pilgrim staff of Tannhäuser. And I will tell you of a flower that grew and withered as suddenly as these, and which expressed a mystic purity by its snowy petals, though its birth was not " of the womb of morning dew," nor its " conception of the glorious prime "; but the juices that fed it were of blood-red wine, rich as the soil that lay in Isabella's pot of basil.

Waerferth was Bishop of Worcester in the reign of the great Alfred, at whose request he translated **the** " Dialogues of Pope Gregory " **into** English. The book has never been put into print, but remains in handwriting in the famous book-houses of Oxenford.

Waerferth **was** a good and learned man, but he loved much sleep and worldly lore ; to talk with his friends about a bright fire of ashen billets, to hear the harp touched, and to drink the wine which chapmen brought hither from the kingdom of the Franks, because the wine-berries did not ripen well in English land. Waerferth loved also his wife Angharad ; for, before the coming of the Norman, bishop and mass-priest were not ashamed of their manhood, but took the comfort and love of woman in holy wedlock. But the haughty French prelates scorn the Word of God, which says that **a** bishop shall be the husband of one wife. Neither would Waerferth shave his face like the womanish ecclesiastics of these days, but let his yellow beard cover his rosy cheeks. Angharad was a Welsh woman, and by some she was accounted **a** sorceress. But I think this **was** only **by** reason of her dark favor and **of** her shape, which was so long and slender that she looked like a snake. It was hard to say whether her eyes were blacker than her eyebrows, or her eyebrows blacker than her hair, which was rolled and piled upon her head in such masses that it seemed a wonder how her thin body could stand so upright under the weight of it. **And** her tire-women reported that when she was unclothed and her hair was

loosened, it would fall about her like a cloak, so
that from her bosom to her feet one might not
see even an inch of her flesh. Withal she was
expert in starcraft, leechdom and wort-cun-
ning. She knew tales of Cynon ap Clydno and
his love, Morvyth, the daughter of Urien; and
of the whitethorn bush in the forest Broch'al-
lean, where Merlin lies chained; and of the
maiden Luned with her enchanted bezel. And
she sang these to her harp in a marvelously
clear, high, and sweet voice, like a wild swan
singing among the rushes of the river Usk, or
upon the solitary lakes of Snowdon. Howbeit,
like all the women of the Bret, she was jealous
and passionate and sharp of tongue, and had a
great pride of lineage. She could—and often
did—recite all the names in her pedigree for
twenty generations, back to a certain king of
the tribe of the Iceni, who had beaten three
Roman legions in battle.

Howbeit, the kinsmen of Waerferth took
offense that he should have to wife a foreign
woman instead of choosing a bride among his
own folk of Wessex; and there was no love lost
between Angharad and them. But it happened
that a distant kinsman, to whom the bishop had
been greatly beholden, died in the capital city
of Winchester, and on his death-bed he com-
mitted his only child, a girl of some seventeen
years, to the care of his cousin Waerferth. The
orphan had neither fee nor land, and the bishop
took her under his protection and into his
household. The maid was well grown and had

eyes as blue as the blossom of the flax and hair
as yellow as a cowslip. Moreover, her ways
were gentle and her voice as soft as a dove's,
and she blushed prettily when spoken to. So
that the women of Waerferth's blood said often
to one another: "It is a pity that our brother
did not get him for a wife some bonny Saxon
wench like Godgifu, instead of that black she-
warlock, who mutters Welsh charms to the
embers when we sit by **her fire, and** whom
Wicglaf the herd has thrice seen floating on the
Severn at midnight in the likeness of a black
cygnet." These speeches were carried to the
ears of Angharad, who forthwith conceived
such hatred and jealousy of her new inmate
that she treated her with the utmost harshness.
One day Waerferth, finding the poor maid in
tears, drew from her, much against her will, an
acknowledgment of Angharad's unkindness.
Thereupon he admonished his wife angrily, saying, " The father of Godgifu was my gossip and
my blood-friend, who saved my life and got me
favor with **the** king. While I have a roof she
shall have shelter, and while I have a loaf she
shall share it. And do not you drive her from the
house, lest evil befall it and the curse of God."
Angharad answered nothing, but her sullen
jealousy waxed daily, and every innocent kindness which her lord showed to his young kins-
woman added proof to his wife's suspicions.
At last she made a desperate resolve and betook
herself to a wise woman of the Cymry who
dwelt by the sea. She found her on a windy

evening, standing by the edge of the waves on a
low sand-spit. She was clad in a single robe of
sea-water green, and was looking off over the
ocean. Her back was turned, and her heel
rested lightly on a rope, the other end of which
was tied to the horns of a monstrous bull which
plunged and bellowed furiously. But such was
the power of the witch that, though she did not
once vary her easy attitude, or even seem to
notice the creature's violent struggles to free
itself, the rope held. When Angharad had
made known her errand, the sorceress, without
turning to face her, threw over her shoulder a
small vial made of the tip of a wild buffalo's
horn and filled with a colorless liquid. Angharad picked it up from the sand where it had
fallen, and kissing the hem of the wise woman's
robe, which was blowing about in the wind, stole
softly away. That evening in his low-studded,
oaken-ceiled hall, blackened by the smoke of
torches, the bishop sat drinking his wine and
listening to his lady as she struck the harp and
sang. She had made herself exceeding fair,
having put on a gown of yellow satin and shoes
of variegated leather, clasped with golden bosses
in the shape of dragons. Ever and anon Waerferth kissed her as he drank, and called for
another song, and ever she sang wildly well.
At last her lord, as was his wont, fell into a
gentle doze, and, with a quick motion, she flung
the witch's poison into the half empty cup and
still played on. And ever her voice was shriller
and louder, as she sang the death-wail of

Aneurin over the warriors who came not back
from Cattraeth, and the lament of Owain when
the drinking-horn, " Hirlas, rich with ancient
silver," was borne to the empty seat of Tudur.

The moonshine, which poured in a flood
through the casement, fell upon the crystal
goblet standing before her sleeping lord, and the
shadow of the wine made a rosy spot in the
white slab of **light** that lay across the board.
Suddenly there was a disturbance in the depths
of the cup. The liquor, glowing like a car-
buncle in its stillness, began to bubble and
seethe, and finally from its agitated surface
there slowly rose and unfolded a great white
flower with **a** golden heart, resembling a lily,
only **that no** lily sprung from earth was ever
half so white or half so beautiful. The lady
stared a moment with dilated eyes upon the
lovely miracle as it glittered in the moon, then,
with a happy cry, threw herself upon her husband's breast. The harp fell with a musical
clang to the floor, and the cup, overturned
by Angharad's sleeve, rolled upon the table.
" What! little wife, have I slept?" said Waerferth, awakening and flinging his arms about
her. And Godgifu, coming at the instant to
the door and lifting the curtain, smiled when she
saw the pair embracing, and retreated softly
without having been perceived. But later,
when the torches were lighted, the goblet lay
upon its side, **but** the wondrous bloom had
vanished. Nor was the table wet or stained
near by, for the flower had drawn up all the

wine into itself, even as the new leaves and buds of the tree draw up the sap in spring. Only a few black seeds, like the seeds of the Lily of the Annunciation, adhered to the bottom of the cup. " This wine draws muddy and near the lees," said the bishop, as he glanced into the empty beaker. " Here are some grape seeds. I must have Wulfheard broach the other cask."

THE END.

JEROME K. JEROME'S NOVEL NOTES.

With **140 half-tone illustrations**, 12mo,
cloth, **$1.25.**

"**AND FLUNG IT IN THE FIRE.**"

Thought to **be the** author's best work. It
does for the novelist's world what " Stage-
land " did for the actor's, containing much
delightful burlesque of the tendencies of
modern fiction. Displays a marked power
in the handling of the grotesque and terrible.